Senior Dreams Can Come True

Jane Claypool Miner

SCHOLASTIC INC.
New York Toronto London Auckland Sydney Tokyo

ISBN 0-590-33180-9

12 11 10 9 8 7 6 5 4 3 2 1   2   5 6 7 8 9/8 0/9

Senior Dreams Can Come True

A Wildfire Book

WILDFIRE® TITLES FROM SCHOLASTIC

I'm Christy by Maud Johnson
Beautiful Girl by Elisabeth Ogilvie
Superflirt by Helen Cavanagh
Dreams Can Come True by Jane Claypool Miner
I've Got a Crush on You by Carol Stanley
An April Love Story by Caroline B. Cooney
Yours Truly, Love Janie by Ann Reit
The Summer of the Sky-Blue Bikini by Jill Ross Klevin
The Best of Friends by Jill Ross Klevin
Second Best by Helen Cavanagh
Take Care of My Girl by Carol Stanley
Secret Love by Barbara Steiner
Nancy & Nick by Caroline B. Cooney
Senior Class by Jane Claypool Miner
Too Young To Know by Elisabeth Ogilvie
Junior Prom by Patricia Aks
He Loves Me Not by Caroline Cooney
Good-bye, Pretty One by Lucille S. Warner
Just a Summer Girl by Helen Cavanagh
Write Every Day by Janet Quin-Harkin
Christy's Choice by Maud Johnson
The Wrong Boy by Carol Stanley
The Boy for Me by Jane Claypool Miner
Class Ring by Josephine Wunsch
Phone Calls by Ann Reit
Just You and Me by Ann Martin
Homecoming Queen by Winifred Madison
Holly in Love by Caroline B. Cooney
Spring Love by Jennifer Sarasin
No Boys? by McClure Jones
Blind Date by Priscilla Maynard
That Other Girl by Conrad Nowels
Little Lies by Audrey Johnson
Broken Dreams by Susan Mendonca
Love Games by Deborah Aydt
Miss Perfect by Jill Ross Klevin
On Your Toes by Terry Morris
Christy's Love by Maud Johnson
Nice Girls Don't by Caroline B. Cooney
Christy's Senior Year by Maud Johnson
Kiss and Tell by Helen Cavanagh
The Boy Next Door by Vicky Martin
Angel by Helen Cavanagh
Out of Bounds by Eileen Hehl
Senior Dreams Can Come True by Jane Claypool Miner

One

Ellynne Aleese slept till almost noon, reveling in her summer vacation freedom. When she woke, she realized she had missed almost half of the most perfect day she'd ever seen. Pulling on her swimsuit as she listened to the news on the radio, she heard the forecast for the day, ". . . 78 degrees at the beaches and rising to the mid 80's. . . ." She decided not to miss another minute of her glorious summer vacation but to treat herself to breakfast at the beach.

In the year she'd lived in her oceanfront Redondo Beach condominium, Ellynne had learned to love the two piers that stretched from the beach to the Pacific Ocean just below the building where she shared an apartment with her mother.

When they'd moved to California from Ohio, Ellynne had no idea how attached she would become to the Pacific Ocean and the coastline. She never tired of looking at the infinite expanse of water and the wonderful sailboats that bobbed around on it. She loved getting up early enough to see the surfers who rode the waves before the beach was closed to them at nine a.m., and she loved watching the people who parked on the beach below her building.

Though many of their neighbors deplored the number of tourists that the pier brought and the traffic on Sundays, Ellynne liked to walk up and down the pier, especially on Sunday afternoons when it was crowded with tourists and she could hear people talking in many different languages, including some that she had identified as Spanish, Chinese, Japanese, and Samoan.

To Ellynne, California was still a Wonderland and she was always amused when her friends and neighbors complained, especially when they complained about the weather. She and her mother had moved to California just before school started last year and she was still getting used to all the changes in her life. Ohio had been very different, not only because she was now living in the world's most perfect climate, but because her own life had changed so much.

Last year had been a year of dreams coming true for Ellynne. Now she was no longer the shy, chubby girl she had been in Ohio, but slim and popular and dating the nicest boy in school, who also happened to be a football hero. The changes had come so fast after she'd lost thirty pounds and moved to Redondo Beach that there were times when Ellynne had to remind herself it had all happened to her. Even her mother's new career as a law student was a startling change; she had been a housewife until Ellynne's father died and she went back to college.

My life is like the ocean, Ellynne thought as she pulled the blinds in her bedroom to prevent the powerful western sun from fading her Grandmother Aleese's wedding quilt. *It changes all the time.*

She made sure that the door was double-locked — the need for tight security was one of the more unpleasant aspects of living in Redondo Beach — and almost ran down the condominium stairs to the boardwalk below. Once on the beach, she paused and drew in the smells and sounds of the day. The air was dry today and the salty smell of the sea didn't seem as strong as usual, but Ellynne could smell the sun hitting the concrete, and the food odors from the pier restaurants called out to her. She decided to celebrate her first day of summer vacation by combining lunch and breakfast into a big feast, something she seldom did, since she was so careful about not finding that thirty pounds she'd lost the summer before.

As she walked toward the pier, she was aware that several people turned to look at her in her bright red bikini. She was glad that her body was as slim as it was; even if she hadn't won the cheerleader competition last year, the exercise had paid off in a really trim figure. *And by the end of the summer, I'll be absolutely brown,* Ellynne promised herself.

She laughed aloud as she remembered what Willie had said about her summer plans. "Your idea of a really good summer seems to be to cook yourself into my coloring. Well sweetie, I can tell you that brown may be beautiful but it makes life a little harder."

Willie was her best friend at Redondo High, the person who had first made it a point to help Ellynne feel at home in her new school. Later Willie, who was head cheerleader, had done everything she could to help Ellynne win the competition and she had been even more disappointed than Ellynne had been when she lost.

Now that the school year was over, Ellynne could see that last year was an almost total success and she was planning new dreams for her senior year. These dreams included getting good grades so she could get a college scholarship and signing up for the drill team. Though cheerleading would have been a triumph, there was nothing wrong with using her newly developed talents in the expert marching squad. Even though she wouldn't be a star in a group of fifty girls, she knew she would enjoy it.

She and Willie had talked over her plans, as they talked over nearly everything, including Willie's decision to take a summer job at the plant nursery where her folks were the best customers. "I'm almost sure they gave the job to me because they felt so guilty about taking all my folks' hard-earned money."

Willie was going to put in as many hours as she could to save money for college despite the fact that her parents were very well off. Her education plans were ambitious and Willie believed her experience as a gardener's assistant would help her in her plans to become a scientist.

Ellynne knew she would miss Willie that summer but they could probably do some things in the evenings once Willie got used to her job. When Ellynne had announced that she intended to spend her whole summer just enjoying the beach, Willie said, "Count me out. I get too sunburned. A lot of white people think that black people don't get sun-burned, but that's not true. And it hurts." But even if Willie wouldn't go to the beach with her, she would probably go to the movies, shopping at the mall, and maybe even do some sightseeing on weekends if Ellynne's money held out. Ellynne planned to spend some of the interest she was earning on the small inheritance she'd been left by her father. The principle was set aside for college, but the interest was hers to use.

Kip had teased her a lot about that when he learned of her summer plans. "If I'd known you were an heiress, I'd have been easier to catch," he said.

When she'd pretended to be mad and thrown a sofa pillow at him, he'd caught her in his arms and kissed her. They'd still been kissing when her mother came in from school that evening. Ellynne had been amused at her mother's clear relief when she'd learned that Kip had a job at Disneyland and would be gone for all of the summer. Obviously her mother was worried that she would get too serious about Kip; but then her mother was worried about a lot of things. She and Ellynne had had another of their major arguments about Ellynne's summer plans, or as her mother put it, her "lack of plans."

Kip had been worried about Ellynne's freedom too. He said he hoped she wouldn't fall in love with someone else while he was "sweating it out in Orange County."

"I won't even find anyone to date," Ellynne predicted. "I'll just walk on the beach and talk to the sea gulls. Besides, there are millions of pretty girls working at Disneyland."

"I'll be too busy sweeping up the top of the Matterhorn," Kip said.

But at her mother's insistence, they'd agreed to give each other a "summer vacation" on going steady. Ellynne supposed she might go out on a few dates if anyone asked her just to keep peace with her mother, but the last thing she wanted was a new boyfriend. Kip was right for her, especially since he'd definitely decided to go to El

Camino Junior College next fall and continue to live at home. That meant they could see a lot of each other; she wasn't sure she would be happy dating someone who was as far away as Willie's boyfriend Carl was. During the year he studied at Stanford and this summer, instead of coming home, he'd gone to Europe for a summer session in languages.

"It's what I get for falling in love with a genius," Willie had said philosophically. "And I'll be busy at my job anyway."

Despite everyone's predictions, Ellynne knew she wasn't going to be bored this summer; she was going to study hard so she could get a head start on her senior year. Except for that, she planned to spend most of her summer just relaxing and enjoying the sun. In a way this would be her last free summer and she was determined to enjoy it, even if everyone else she knew was working hard and expected her to be miserable. She suspected her biggest fight would be against guilt, not loneliness.

As the thoughts roamed through her brain, Ellynne's nose led her to Pete's at the end of the straight pier. She could smell the coffee and fried potatoes from outside and she knew from experience that the food would be good. Besides, Pete's was so filled with other beachgoers that she wouldn't feel funny in her swimsuit. A lot of the restaurants on the pier were dress-up places and they had signs on the doors that said things like, *Shoes and Shirts Please*, but the only sign on Pete's said *"Breakfast Served 24 Hours."*

There were no empty tables so Ellynne sat at the counter. As she ordered steak and eggs, whole wheat toast, orange juice, and coffee, a very tall, very handsome young man came in the door. Though there were lots of empty stools, he sat down beside her and smiled as he asked, "Through with the menu?"

Ellynne handed him the menu and smiled back. He seemed like a friendly person and, to tell the truth, she was somewhat dazzled by his good looks. His eyes were a startling shade of blue — a sort of light gray-blue that, instead of being pale, was very bright. His skin was tanned a deep gold, the color that Ellynne had come to think of as the ideal California blond color. It occurred to her that he might be a movie star or model, he was so perfect-looking. But would a movie star sit on a stool in a restaurant like Pete's?

The dark golden skin, light eyes, and height were complemented by his pale blond hair and muscular body. But instead of being one of those overly muscled body builders that Ellynne sometimes saw working out on the beach, this young man had long, strong, smooth muscles. What made him dazzling, though, was his smile. He had the whitest, most even teeth she had ever seen and his smile was as warm and open as the sunshine.

"Another day in paradise," he said.

Ellynne wasn't sure whether she should reply or not. There were a lot of very peculiar people in Southern California, especially along the beach. Her mother was always warning her that they weren't in Ohio anymore and that she had to be careful. She *was* careful — she was usually with one of her friends when she ate in restaurants. But this summer she was going to be on her own. If she was going to have any fun at all, she would have to be free to talk to a few people. Being scared all the time wasn't very smart either.

"I was talking about the weather, not calling you an angel," the young man said. He was smiling now, as though he found her hesitation funny.

"It *is* a beautiful day," Ellynne agreed.

The waitress brought her breakfast and the young man ordered coffee. Ellynne realized he had probably only asked for the menu to start a conversation with her. Since he had also chosen to sit beside her, she guessed he was probably trying to flirt; the idea pleased her but also made her feel self-conscious. His next words were, "I like a girl with a healthy appetite."

Ellynne bit into her toast and tried not to smile as she chewed. When she didn't respond, he added, "A lot of girls don't eat anything at all. I like to see a girl enjoy herself. That's what life is really about, isn't it? You look like you're having a good time right now."

"I am," Ellynne admitted. She wasn't sure what else to say so she ate steadily and tried to look noncommittal. The steak was tough and the eggs were kind of cold but she kept eating because she was hungry and she didn't want him to guess that his conversation and the fact that he was looking at her were making her self-conscious. While it was kind of fun to have a handsome young man try to pick her up on the first day of her vacation, she was also beginning to figure out that there might be some problems with doing things alone all summer.

"Hey look, I'm not your ordinary pervert or anything," he said. "I'm just trying to be friendly. I've seen you around some and I thought this was a good chance to get acquainted. You live in that condo with the red iron balconies, don't you?"

"Yes I do," Ellynne answered. "Do you go to Redondo High?"

He laughed at the idea and shook his head. "Sorry about that. It finished me some time ago. I am a student though, if that makes me more respectable. I'm at El Camino."

That did make him more respectable, Ellynne decided. Though her mother would say she had no business trusting strangers, even handsome ones, she was fairly certain that he really was what he said he was, a college student who'd seen her and wanted to get acquainted.

She relaxed a bit. "I'm kind of new at school and a lot of people know me who I don't know yet. I thought you looked too old but you never can tell. Some seniors are nineteen."

"I'm twenty," he said. Then he added, "I see you on the beach. You usually run in the mornings and walk in the evenings. Your favorite time of day is sunset and you can sit very still, watching the sun go down. They say that the ability to sit very still is a sign of great spiritual advancement." Then he laughed and explained, "I'm not a religious freak but I have a lot of friends who do yoga. Some of them talk a lot and others just stretch. The talkers try harder to teach but you learn more from the stretchers."

"I do like the sunsets," Ellynne said, smiling at him. "They seem a little like movie sets to someone from Ohio. I suppose I'll get used to them eventually though."

"How long you been here?"

"A year."

He laughed and said, "You're practically a native."

"Are you?"

"A native?"

"Yes."

"Yes, but I'm not used to the sunsets. I lived behind a hill when I was a kid and didn't really begin to look at things till I started hanging out on the beach."

"Do you spend a lot of time on the beach?" Ellynne thought she wasn't doing very well with her end of the conversation, but he talked very differently than most of the boys she knew. Kip, for instance, was a predictable person who talked about solid things like school and sports. With Kip she never felt foolish anymore, but she was sorry to discover that she hadn't completely kicked the shyness habit with handsome strangers.

"I more or less live at the beach," he said.

"You don't work?"

"I'm very wealthy though," he assured her with great seriousness. "I've got the wind, the moon, and the stars. Right?"

"How about the sun?" She decided she liked him, partly because he'd just told her practically the same thing she'd told her mother during their big argument about how she would spend her summer. This guy obviously knew how to enjoy himself.

"Sun belongs to everyone," he answered her question.

When she didn't add anything, he said, "I feel really alive when I'm near the ocean."

"I read once that people who live near the ocean develop a necessity for the salt air. It has something to do with the ions in the ozone level," Ellynne said.

He was smiling at her. Had she made herself seem as foolish as she felt? "Something like that," he said. "Did you know we have on matching swimsuits?"

She saw that he was wearing a bright red suit, exactly the same red as hers. "I hadn't noticed," she admitted.

"We also look alike," he said. "Same

coloring, same suits. Do you think it means anything?"

Her hair was a honey-gold color and her eyes were a deeper blue, but she supposed they might pass for relatives. Actually, their features weren't that much alike; his nose was perfectly straight, and his brows were heavy and straight. He looked a lot more like Brooke Shields's twin than hers but Ellynne decided not to get into any discussion of appearances at all. She ignored his question and asked, "Do you usually go to the beach by my house? Is that why you see me?"

"Avenue C," he answered.

He gave the name of a section of the sand that was called after a street that led to the beach. Ellynne knew that the streets began with the A B C's about two miles from the pier. She also knew that she must have walked by his spot on the beach many times. How could she have missed anyone as handsome as he was? It was hard not to stare at him.

"My name's Kenny. Look, you going to be around all summer?"

"Yes." Why was her heart pounding like this? Just because he'd sat beside her? That wasn't like her usual sensible self.

"We all hang out there, on Avenue C. Want to come down?"

"Who's we?"

"Just a bunch of people. Friends. All respectable." Then he added, "Some are your age. Not all old guys like me. Want to come?"

She hadn't told him her age so she supposed he meant some were in high school. What would he think if he knew she was only fifteen? She wouldn't be sixteen for a couple of months despite the fact that she was a senior in high school. But she told herself that most of her friends were older than she was and that a twenty-year-old college student was really no different from a nineteen-year-old college student. That was what Kip would be in a month. Besides, he'd only invited her to come to the beach, not to go out or anything. She took a deep breath and asked, "You mean today?"

"Sure, why not?"

Ellynne thought it over as she chewed the last bit of rubbery steak. How could it possibly hurt to walk down to Avenue C and meet his friends? Maybe they would be just what she needed to make her summer one she could really remember all her life.

"Sure," she said, "that sounds like fun."

Two

The boardwalk led from the beginning of the pier all the way to Torrance Beach, about five miles away. Ellynne knew the coastline by heart because she'd walked or run that five miles many times, but she'd never actually sat on any of the beaches except the one closest to her house. From what she'd learned at school, certain beach locations were unofficially reserved for certain social groups; she knew that some of the football players and their girlfriends spent a lot of time at Torrance Beach but she'd only been there twice for evening beach parties. Both times it had been cold, and she and Kip had left early.

Now, as she walked beside Kenny, she wished she'd spent more time actually lying on the beach because she was fairly sure that his friends would have the same glorious tans that he did. Until now, most of her beach time was spent in solitary exercising in the early morning and late afternoon and her tan, though respectable for so early in the year, was certainly not spectacular.

Kenny was riding a bicycle, so she was walking as fast as she could while he pedaled as slowly as he could. He had offered her a ride on his handlebars but she had turned him down quickly, pointing out that it was against the law.

Now he asked, "You always obey the law?"

"More or less."

"Is that a policy of yours or just laziness?"

She couldn't tell from his voice whether he was teasing her or not and since he was slightly ahead of her, she couldn't look at his face to get a clue. What she could see was his strong, broad shoulders and the muscles that moved sensuously just below the surface of that golden skin. She decided she might as well give him a serious answer. "I don't have a lot of opportunity to break laws but I'm pretty honest anyway. I don't cheat on tests, for instance."

He stopped his bike abruptly and turned to face her. He lifted his sunglasses to his forehead and his blue eyes looked almost silver in the bright sun. "I just want to look in the eyes of someone who can honestly say she's never cheated on a test in her life. Can you say that? Honestly?"

He leaned his head forward and looked directly into her eyes, staring without blinking as he moved his head closer and closer. Though unsmiling, Ellynne knew he had to be teasing her. She lifted her sunglasses and tried to stare back for a moment but his gaze was too riveting. She blinked and laughed.

He laughed even louder and said, "I knew you couldn't be that pure."

"But I am." Ellynne was sputtering with laughter now. "I *don't* cheat on tests."

"Then why are you laughing?" His voice was a mock growl.

"I'm not laughing," she answered. The effort required to control her laughter made her laugh even harder. To distract him, she started running ahead.

He quickly passed her and then doubled back. For the next few blocks, they traveled in that manner, with her running and him circling her on his bicycle. As they passed the Knob Hill steps and moved toward Avenue A, she slowed down. He slowed down beside her and asked, "You have a bike?"

"Sure."

"You'll need it if you're going to hang out with us this summer. Can't have you taking a bus every time you want a sandwich or a glass of milk, can we?"

She was surprised that he seemed to be assuming that she would be spending the summer with him and his friends. He didn't seem to be one of those people who came on so strong that they frightened you away. Except that he seemed so sure that they would be friends, he seemed easy-going and nice. *Laid back.* That was a word that described Kenny very well, she decided.

"You surf?" he asked.

Ellynne shook her head. She'd hoped to try it when she first moved to California but she'd been too shy to go to the beach alone much last summer. None of the friends she'd made at school surfed. While a lot of kids at Redondo High did surf, most of them were in a different social group and Ellynne hadn't gotten very well acquainted with any of them. She had the definite impression that being a surfer meant a lot more than owning a board, that it involved a set of attitudes toward life. Most of the surfers seemed a lot more interested in partying and living the good life than worrying about the future.

She found she was looking forward to meeting Kenny's friends and was pleased to discover that much of her shyness really had disappeared during the last year. Part of her self-confidence came from knowing she looked just fine in her red bikini, part of it came from knowing that she was accepted by her old friends already.

"Body surf?" Kenny asked.

"What's the difference?"

Kenny laughed so loud she thought he might fall off his bike, which was moving too slowly to be safe anyway. Ellynne began to get very annoyed and she said, "Supercilious behavior will only offend."

That made him laugh even louder but he

asked, "Where'd you get an expression like that? Your English teacher?"

"Math," Ellynne admitted. "But I hate being laughed at and I don't think it's nice for you to make fun of me just because I'm not a California native." She loved California but she hated those bumper stickers that said *California Native.* In fact, she thought Californians were entirely too conscious of where a person happened to be born.

"Lots of natives can't even swim," Kenny said. "You do swim, don't you?"

"Of course." She didn't tell him that she'd learned to swim in a pool and hadn't really ventured into the ocean beyond wading in the surf or paddling around in the little beach beside the pier where the surf was almost nonexistent. It wasn't exactly that she was afraid to swim in the ocean, it was just that she didn't know how to begin.

"You look athletic," he said. "Like you might do more than just decorate the beach. But I guess that comes from running."

"Partly," Ellynne said. She wasn't sure she wanted to tell him about the long hours she'd spent practicing to be a cheerleader. Though she'd made her peace with it, she didn't like admitting that she'd been defeated.

"We're here," Kenny said. He hopped off his bike and walked it down some short steps onto the sand. Then he leaned the bike against the steps and walked toward a group of people who were sitting on the sand. Ellynne felt very awkward as she followed him but she had come this far, so it would have felt even sillier not to join them.

There were three young men who were sitting in a sort of circle, talking to each other as they drank orange juice from plastic bottles. As Kenny walked by, they looked up and nodded but he passed them by, as he did the other group of three girls who were lying on towels with their faces to the sun. Ellynne guessed that most of them were older than she was and that they spent a lot of time on the beach because they all had tans that they had to have started around Easter.

Kenny crossed one foot over the other and sat down in one swift motion. He chose a spot on the edge of a blue beach towel that was mostly covered by a very tanned blonde in a white one-piece swimsuit with a deep, deep V in the back. The blonde kicked her feet a little when Kenny dropped some sand on her legs and didn't even lift her head as she mumbled, "Kenny? You seen Sailor?"

"Nope," Kenny answered. He looked at Ellynne and smiled as he motioned to her to sit down on the empty bright yellow towel beside the blue one. He said, "This is Choo-Choo. She doesn't talk before noon, she sleeps."

ChooChoo rolled her head from one side to the other but said nothing. Kenny was still sitting cross-legged on the blue towel and he motioned again for Ellynne to use the yellow one. She said, "I can't just take someone's towel."

"You really are honest, aren't you?"

"I was going to have breakfast, then walk. I don't usually just lie down on the sand or else I would have brought my own towel."

"The towel's mine," Kenny said, "at least I think it is."

Ellynne sat down on the yellow towel and stretched her legs out in front of her. She said, "It's past noon. I think it's about one o'clock."

Kenny leaned over and tickled ChooChoo under the ribs. As he did so, he managed to hug her. "Hear that, ChooChoo? Time to get up."

He pulled the girl off the towel, turning her around, sitting her up as though she were a rag doll; she didn't seem to be enjoying his roughhousing much and her first words were, "He said he'd be here by ten."

Kenny turned to Ellynne and said, "Sailor's her best buddy. Mine, too. We're rivals, aren't we ChooChoo?"

The girl seemed very tired and her face looked strange because she had deep sand marks impressed on one cheek where she'd been sleeping. Even so Ellynne could see that she was absolutely beautiful. She had large black eyes, a full mouth and high cheekbones. Ellynne saw that much of her deep color was natural and she was probably a mix of some exotic group of ancestors, though Ellynne couldn't guess whether they were Asian or Latin American. Though ChooChoo was naturally very beautiful, it was the absolutely straw-colored hair, cut to only about an inch at the top, that made her so unusual looking.

ChooChoo didn't seem very happy with Kenny and ignored Ellynne altogether. When Kenny said, "I want you to see my new girl. Make friends, you know," the girl just nodded to Ellynne and turned to the radio on the edge of her towel. She changed the station and lay back down, this time staring straight up at the sun and repeating, "He said he'd be early today."

Just when Ellynne was sure that Kenny had something going with the beautiful girl, he seemed to lose interest in her totally and turned back to Ellynne, asking, "You aware you haven't told me your name? How can you be my girl if you haven't got a name?"

"I've got a name and I'm not your girl." She was wondering what he would say next. Was Kenny going to turn out to be one of those guys who could only relate by making jokes? Though she was still startled by how good-looking he was, she was not the least bit afraid of him; he seemed like a kid a lot of the time. She had to admit he'd made her laugh and she'd had fun with him so far, but it was hard to take him seriously. She thought of Kip, who was such a hardworking, determined person. How could two people, Kip and Kenny, grow up in the same community and be so different?

"I have a boyfriend, someone I'm really close to, but he's working all summer. In fact, all my friends are working. I want to relax and enjoy myself, so when I met you, I thought it might be nice to have a friend, to meet a group of people who were enjoying the beach and stuff. . . ." Her voice trailed off and she wondered if she'd said too much. She really didn't want to frighten him away but she wanted to be honest. She added, "I have a feeling we're really different kinds of people. I usually spend most of my time working or studying and I plan a lot. I have a feeling you live a different kind of life."

Kenny seemed to hear what she had to say because he nodded and said, "O.K., so you're not my girl. We're just good friends, like they say in the gossip columns." Then he switched into one of his funny faces and turned to her, asking, "But just tell me what's wrong with me and I'll change it. You don't like my teeth? I'll get braces. You want dark hair? I can dye it. I consider myself supremely fixable. Place your order. What's your name?"

"Ellynne. Ellynne Aleese."

"Sounds like something you eat, like Orville Swartchkoph's popcorn or Harvey Wallboard ice cream."

Why was she laughing at him? Was it because he was trying so hard or was it because it had been so long since she'd really had someone who knew how to enjoy life? When she and Lizzie had been little girls back in Ohio, they'd had a lot of silly games, but she was in a different place now and her life seemed so much more serious. Even her mother had changed since Ohio. . . .

"Did I say something wrong? You don't want to be an ice-cream cone? What happened? What did I do wrong?"

He tossed sand on her legs and she felt he really wanted to know so she answered, "I guess I was just thinking about life. You know, what's it all about? I mean, I was thinking that I'm sort of planning to waste the summer and all my friends and my mother think I should be working."

"Work?" Kenny jumped up, raised his arms and pretended to be flailing them about in madness. "You just said the one word that drives me criminally insane. Don't ever say that word to me again."

He was making madman faces at her and she was laughing so hard that she couldn't stop. Then he pulled her up and said, "I think we ought to take a little swim, just to wash off the ugly stench of the word. Washing off the work ethic, that's what we call it. Come on."

Ellynne tried not to let her timidity show as she followed Kenny out to the water, but when he ran and dived in, she recoiled from the first shock of the cold. Unlike lakes, she knew the ocean would never be any warmer and she told herself if she was going to enjoy her summer, she might as well get used to it.

She took a deep breath and started wading out toward the waves.

The surf was small and she was glad of that because she'd never figured out what you were supposed to do when the waves crashed over you. She could see that Kenny was already through the breaking line of the waves and swimming straight out to sea. She stood on the shoreline and let the waves run up to her, splashing over her as they broke. One or two seemed very powerful and almost knocked her down, but she knew they were almost nonwaves compared to most days. What must it feel like to really be in high surf? She'd seen pictures of body surfers in ten- or twelve-foot waves but she couldn't imagine the experience.

Kenny kept swimming straight out, until he seemed like a small dot on the horizon. Ellynne gradually moved past the breaking line, enjoying the feel of the sand slipping away under her feet as the waves crashed against her. Eventually, she was off her feet, swimming in the ocean and she headed beyond the breakers, swimming a few feet and then turning to swim sideways. Since she didn't want to get into a situation she couldn't handle, she kept close to the shoreline.

The salty water burned her face a bit and she tasted it several times. While it didn't make her eyes as red as the chlorine of a swimming pool, it did burn. Yet there was an extra buoyancy to her body and the smells were new and pleasant. She loved the feel of the cold water on her body and the heat of the sun on her face at first, but she soon discovered she was really cold and headed for the shore.

Even though the surf was very small, she felt glad that she'd braved it. For Ellynne, it had been the best start she could hope for and she was glad that she hadn't been forced to begin in really strong waves. She dropped back down on the yellow towel and stretched out, turning her face upward and closing her eyes. It felt wonderful to let the sun dry her off and she could feel the salt tightening her skin as it evaporated.

She was almost dozing when she felt the sharp pricks of cold water dropping on her. She was startled and sat up quickly, as Kenny shook himself like a dog, spraying water all over her. She laughed but Choo-Choo, who had also been sprayed, snarled, "Hey, quit it." Then ChooChoo stood up, glared at Kenny and said, "You're standing on my towel."

"Sorry," Kenny said and stepped off. ChooChoo folded her blue towel in swift motions of anger and then turned to Ellynne and said, "You're sitting on my towel."

Ellynne jumped up, stammering, "I'm sorry, I didn't know it was yours." She tried to fold it up.

ChooChoo smiled and shook her head and said, "It's not your fault. You'd better go home too. You're really red." Then she turned to Kenny and said, "Tell Sailor to call me when he gets the time."

Ellynne watched as ChooChoo walked across the beach to the steps and then she said, "I guess I'll go too."

"Day's early," Kenny said.

Ellynne shook her head. "We don't even have towels. I wish you had told me it was hers."

Kenny shrugged and grinned. "I thought it might be mine."

"I'd better go."

"I'll walk you home."

"What about Sailor?"

"What about him?"

"You're supposed to give him a message."

"He'll get by."

"I thought he was your best friend?"

Kenny seemed to think that over for a minute and then he said, "I'll tell *them* to tell him." He pointed out to the ocean where the three fellows who had been sitting beside them were now swimming. He cupped his hands and shouted to the sea, "Tell Sailor to call ChooChoo."

The girls who had been there earlier were already gone. Though there were several towels spread around, if she and Kenny left, there wouldn't be anyone around until the three guys returned. Ellynne wished Kenny had told her some of his friends' names but she figured if she came back often enough, she would learn them.

If I come back, Ellynne said to herself. She wasn't sure yet whether she would but being with Kenny had been a lot more fun than spending the day alone. She'd told him about Kip so she wasn't playing games or anything. Besides, a guy as good-looking as Kenny could look out for himself. It wasn't as if she was taking advantage of him. But it was time to go now; her skin was burning and she was tired. She wanted to take a shower and start dinner before her mother got home from school.

"I have to go now," Ellynne said. "I'll see you tomorrow."

"Tomorrow, if the surf's up, I'll teach you how to bodysurf."

"In one day?" Ellynne laughed.

"Nope," Kenny said, "we've got lots of time."

"The whole summer," Ellynne agreed.

"Forever."

She was a little surprised that he'd dropped back into that corny, romantic stuff since he'd been treating her like a friend for most of the day. As she walked away, Ellynne realized that his "forever" reply had to do with time on the beach, not any romance between them. Kenny was obviously not measuring his life into vacation and work time; today had been normal life for him, not a special treat. Ellynne wondered if he was as happy as he seemed. What would a life like his really feel like?

T_hree_

Dinner was late and her mother was annoyed as they sat down at the table. Judith Aleese looked at the salad and hamburgers with distaste and said, "Having a resident cook certainly didn't improve the menu."

"I guess it does look kind of bad," Ellynne apologized. "I'll do better tomorrow."

"Tomorrow I'll be gone till ten," her mother reminded her. "It's my Tuesday night horror show."

"Still having trouble with Dr. Callahan?" Ellynne sympathized. She knew her mother would cheer up if she could get her to start talking about law school and her ambitious plans for finishing three years in two. Ellynne knew her mother was having a great time in school, but the hours were long and the stress was great.

Her mother sighed and said, "Pete Callahan is brilliant but he's also cantankerous, opinionated, and a pain in the. . . . Pass the mustard please."

They laughed and the rest of their dinner was pleasant. After dinner Judith brought the subject back to her concern that Ellynne wasn't making the most of the summer. *Incipient hedonism* was what Judith called Ellynne's plan to do nothing. That had sent Ellynne to the dictionary to look up both words. She'd found that incipient meant beginning and hedonism was an old philosophical school of thought that believed that pleasure was the major reason for living.

"And how was your first day as a practicing hedonist?" Judith asked.

Ignoring the barb, Ellynne answered, "Fine. I met some friends and spent the day with them. I went swimming and had breakfast on the pier."

"Your face looks like it belongs in the tank at the Lobster House," her mother said. "I thought we agreed you'd use sunscreen this summer?"

"I will," Ellynne promised. She wanted to avoid another row with Judith if she could but her mother seemed to be in one of her moods.

"What about your reading? Did you study today?"

"Mother, it was the first day of vacation."

"That was the agreement, young lady. You do all the housework and cooking, you study for two hours a day, and you wear sunscreen. Even so, I don't like the idea of your being alone all day long with nothing to do."

It was going to be an exact replay if Ellynne didn't watch out. They'd wrangled over Judith's disapproval for three hours one Saturday morning and finally come up with the compromise. "I promise I'll wear sunscreen tomorrow and study hard and that you'll have something good to eat. Maybe hot dogs?"

Ellynne was still hoping that she could joke enough to jostle her mother out of the bad mood she was in but it clearly wasn't going to work. "I told you I wouldn't be home tomorrow till late. That's what really worries me — you'll have too many hours alone. It's just not good, Ellynne. I know it isn't."

"You're right. One of these days you'll come home and I'll be a brainless vegetable. I can see the headlines now, 'High school coed OD's on sunshine and leisure time.' You know what, Mother, you should try a little fun yourself. It's addictive."

Her mother frowned at her and shook her head. "You never used to talk like that. I wonder if I did the right thing by moving to California. Maybe if you'd stayed in Ohio. . . ."

"Mother, be serious. Kids in Ohio are young too. I don't know why you think California has been so bad for me. I did all right in school last year, didn't I? What's wrong with a 3.6 grade average?"

"It isn't high enough for a scholarship, that's what," her mother snapped. "If I hadn't let you waste your whole year fooling around with that cheerleading nonsense you would have made a 4.0, I'm sure of it. I want you to make something of your life, Ellynne, not just be a foolish teenybopper. I want the best for you."

"You want the best for *yourself*," Ellynne snapped. "That's what it's really all about, you know. You feel like you got a late start in life because of me and Dad and now you want me to make it all up for you. I'm supposed to get a 4.0 because you wish you could have gone to an Ivy League school. I'm supposed to be sensible because you wasted your life on loving Dad and me. I'm supposed to do everything the way you wish you'd done it."

They were standing in the small kitchen, facing each other. The words that tumbled out of their mouths fit as smoothly as though they were lines in a play, they had been spoken so often. Not that they quarreled all the time, Ellynne reminded herself, but they did seem to quarrel a lot lately and it was always over how Ellynne was spending or wasting her time.

"I told you I *do not* regret marrying young," Judith said. "If I hadn't married your father when I did, I wouldn't have had as much time with him as I did but that doesn't mean I want you to live your life the same way. I love you, Ellynne. I want you to be free, free to choose independently and intelligently."

She could have said that her mother had a funny way of encouraging freedom, but that would have continued the pointless argument. They were both tired and discouraged enough as it was. Once again the peacemaker, Ellynne said, "I know you do, Mother, and I know you love me and try to do what's best. But you agreed I could have the summer if I'd study for the fall. Let's not argue anymore and please, don't worry about me. I'm fine, I really am."

Her mother nodded, "I'm sorry. I wish I didn't nag you so much. I know you're a good girl and I'm proud of you but I don't always understand you. I guess you know that." She shook her head, "Sometimes I wonder if you're more like your father than I can remember, but I don't think so. You seem to be different from any of us."

"That's me, the mutant daughter."

"Don't be flip."

Suddenly, Ellynne was very tired of the whole situation; why did her mother make everything into such a big deal? Hadn't she tried to smooth things over? So why did her mother keep correcting her? And what was this about being so different from everyone else in the family? Did her mother really think she was that weird? She wished she was back on the beach with Kenny and his friends. At least there, you could make a joke without having everyone think you were so weird they were ready to disinherit you.

"I guess I'll study," her mother said.

"Maybe you could do the same."

"After I do the dishes," Ellynne agreed. But when the dishes were put away and she went to her bedroom, Ellynne spent almost an hour in the bathtub, soaking in bubble bath and reading a novel. Then she put cream over her whole body, massaging it into her slightly burned skin. She put a lot on her face, hoping that it would take all the redness away so she could safely go back to the beach tomorrow. After she finished doing all that, it was nine o'clock and she decided she was tired enough to go to bed. The sun had drained her energy.

When she lay down and closed her eyes, a lot of the sights and sounds of the beach came back to her. She could almost hear the sea gulls crying and the sunburn was warm enough so that it felt like the sun was still on her skin. She definitely *could* hear the surf pounding against the sand because it was right outside her window. Funny how she lived so close to the ocean and today was the first day that she felt as if she'd experienced it.

The next morning, she woke early and gave the whole apartment a good cleaning before her mother went to school. Judith seemed in a much better mood and was very cheerful as she ate her breakfast and read the newspaper. She looked up at Ellynne cleaning out the refrigerator. "I see the lobster has turned," her mother said.

"What?" Ellynne was confused.

"It was a little joke. The lobster, that's you, has turned. As in worms turning, or new leaves."

"Oh. Do you want me to save this yogurt?"

"What's the date?"

"March 23. I guess not. It's almost July. I wonder what happens to you if you eat old yogurt?"

"Ugh." Her mother shook her head in disgust.

"I wasn't really thinking about eating it," Ellynne said. "I was just speculating. I mean, you read about these old people who live to be a hundred and twenty just because they eat a lot of yogurt. Do you think they eat young yogurt? And if you eat old yogurt you die young?"

Her mother put down the paper and stared at her. "Know what I think? I think the sun got to your brain."

"I'm cleaning house," Ellynne pointed out.

"That's what I mean," her mother folded the paper, carried her plate to the sink, kissed her daughter on the forehead and said, "Have a good day. I'll be home about eleven."

"You have a good day and watch out for Smuggers." It was a half warning, half joke because her mother's school was in downtown Los Angeles, almost forty minutes away from where they lived. When they first moved here, they'd chosen Redondo Beach because just about everyone they met said they couldn't live close to the school because of muggers and smog. They'd coined their own private word to combine the two dangers that people seemed so preoccupied with.

Ellynne finished cleaning house by noon. Telling herself that she could study that evening, she put on her red bikini, rolled some sunscreen up in a towel and headed for the beach. She thought about taking some money in case she got hungry but decided it would just be a lot of bother to carry a coin purse and there were certainly no pockets on her swimsuit.

She walked along the water's edge instead of the boardwalk just for the fun of it. She carried her rubber thongs under her arm for a while and then stopped long enough to roll them inside her towel. Even so, she wished she could figure out some way to travel absolutely without burdens as she walked the three miles from her house to Avenue C beach. It was fun to feel as though she was free of all cares, as though she was absolutely empty of responsibilities. Even the towel, shoes, and sunscreen seemed like a lot to worry about.

The funny part was that she wasn't a bit nervous about seeing Kenny and his friends again. She'd had enough time with him yesterday to feel like she knew him and she was pretty sure he'd be glad to see her. Actually, on her walk down to their spot, she spent her time looking at the wonderful patterns the foamy water made on the sand and enjoying the way the wet sand felt as she pressed her feet over it. Aside from enjoying looking at the other people on the beach, watching a few sea gulls make daring dives into the sea, and smelling the salty air, her mind was completely free of thoughts.

She was having such a good time that she almost overshot her mark. Then she saw one of the guys who'd been there yesterday marching out of the water, lifting his knees high, as though he were doing a German soldier goosestep from an old war movie. When he got closer, Ellynne saw that he was wearing swim fins. As he bent down to take them off, she said, "Hi, Kenny around?"

He looked up, recognized her, and said, "Over there with Sailor and the others." He pointed to the same spot on the sand where they'd been yesterday. When Ellynne turned to walk toward it, he fell into step beside her, saying, "Been practicing my stroke every day. I'm ready for the big ones. Going to Hawaii next week. Ever been?"

"No."

"Been twice. Every time, I try to figure out how to stay. Maybe get a job in a surfing shop or something. I'll find a way because the waves there are the best. One day I did seven aerials before I crashed. Ten foot bowls. It was really radical."

Ellynne had to stop herself from laughing as she realized she hadn't understood one word except he liked Hawaii, though she assumed he was talking about surfing. "My name's Ellynne," she offered.

He nodded. "Saw you yesterday. You surf?"

"Not yet." What had made her say that? Was she actually going to try it?

"I can let you have a thruster cheap if you want to start."

Ellynne had to bite her lip to keep from giggling. Talking to this guy was like talking to someone from outer space. "I'll think about it," she said and turned to Kenny, who was sitting on the same yellow towel she'd used yesterday and talking to a young man who was almost the same shade of golden brown he was but had dark brown, curly hair and a tattoo with an anchor on his arm. She knew it had to be Kenny's friend, Sailor.

Kenny smiled and said, "Glad you got here. We're taking up a collection for food. Got any money?"

"Sorry," Ellynne said, then she asked, "Where shall I spread my towel?"

Kenny didn't seem surprised by the question, though she'd felt awkward asking it. He patted the sand beside him and said, "This is the best spot. I can let you have it for a smile."

Grateful that her welcome had been so easy and complete, Ellynne spread her towel out beside the one that Kenny and Sailor were sitting on. She saw that ChooChoo's towel was beside them, as well as her portable radio, but the girl was nowhere in sight. Ellynne introduced herself to Sailor. "I'm Ellynne," she said.

"Welcome. No money?"

"I'm sorry."

Sailor frowned at the dollar and change in his hand and grumbled, "I'll have to hit ChooChoo again. Makes her mad." He leaned over and picked up a pack of cigarettes from ChooChoo's towel. Ellynne watched as Sailor extracted a five-dollar bill that was folded and neatly tucked between the cellophane and paper wrappings. Then he stood up and said, "I'll do my best."

Sailor walked toward the steps that led to the street. Ellynne asked Kenny, "What's a thruster?"

"A surfboard, why?"

"Your friend offered to sell me a thruster and I didn't even know what it was. He speaks a foreign language."

"Davy? He's sort of obsessed with the subject, I admit. Can't surf though, and you don't want his board. What you should start with is a basic local board. We'll keep our eyes open if you like it. How's your balance?"

"I'm not sure," Ellynne said. "I did pretty well at cheerleading but I didn't get the spot. I'm hoping to get on the drill team next fall. And I'm pretty good on a bicycle."

Kenny laughed. "Cheerleader? I should have known. . . ."

"I'm not sure what that means but I'm positive I don't like it. What if I'd said, 'Surfer? I should have known. . . .'"

"I just meant you're good-looking."

"It sounded like you meant 'good-looking idiot.' Anyway, I didn't make it and I have a 3.6 grade average."

"Touchy, touchy," Kenny admonished. "You don't have to convince me you're intelligent. So relax, you're among friends."

"I guess I am touchy," Ellynne said and lay down on her towel, stretching her arms out over her head and staring up at the blue sky. "I think I feel kind of guilty about wasting the summer."

"How do you know you're wasting it?" Kenny asked.

She turned her head to look at him. He really was handsome and when he smiled, as he was doing right now, he seemed like he knew a lot of special things — almost as if he had a secret he wanted to share. It occurred to her that Kenny was probably quite an intelligent person himself. She smiled and didn't answer his question because she had no answer.

"Actually, I don't think I'm wasting it," Ellynne conceded. "It's just that I'm surrounded by such hard-working people. My mom's in law school and she's really working too hard. My boyfriend has this job at Disneyland where he works ten-hour days, and even my best girlfriend is working from five in the morning until four in the afternoon in a nursery. I guess I feel like I ought to be doing something too."

"You should be protecting yourself," Kenny said in a fake German accent. "It might be catching." Then he switched to his serious voice and said, "Just because you're surrounded by workaholics doesn't mean you have to be one. After all, you're a good-looking seventeen-year-old."

"Fifteen," she said. "I skipped a year in school and I won't be sixteen till the fall." She had learned a lot of things last year and one of them was it was better to be honest about her age and not let it get in her way.

"Fifteen and a senior," Kenny shook his head. "You'd better watch out or you'll have workaholism so bad you'll never be able to kick the habit."

She laughed and said, "I knew you would make my summer more fun."

"Fun." He spoke in a funny doctor's accent. "That's what I prescribe. More fun. Take big doses every day and your cheeks stay rosy."

Ellynne lay back on her towel and smiled at the blue sky. She had been right to make friends with Kenny; he was just what she needed in her life right now. He was a fun guy. Without Kip and Willie around, she needed someone to have fun with. She complimented herself on good judgment. She hadn't just been attracted to his good looks, she had been attracted to his joyful personality.

Later, he brought up the subject of surfing again, asking, "Do you think you'd like to try to learn?"

Ellynne laughed and said, "You'd better

start me on vocabulary lessons first. Anyway, I need to get used to swimming in the ocean before I do anything else."

"Vocabulary's easy enough and it doesn't really help you on a board. I mean, the sea gulls don't talk to you and neither do the waves. Besides, Davy's kind of weird but the rest of us are normal enough. It's not like you're in with a group of really dedicated surfers or anything. I mean, we surf, but we also live. Some of those guys are so into it, they make surfing exactly like work. You know what I mean — going to meets, making reps, first thing you know what was fun turns out to be something on the back of a cereal box."

"Cartoons?" Ellynne asked.

"No," he laughed. "I mean endorsements. Some surfers take a perfectly good sport and turn it into a business. If I wanted to make a business, I'd farm, not surf."

"Farm?"

"Sure, why not?"

"It's just really hard to imagine you on a farm, Kenny."

Kenny nodded his head very seriously, a gesture that Ellynne learned was a signal for him to begin acting in one of his preposterous voices. Sure enough, he made a funny face and began talking with a phony hillbilly accent. "Anyone can farm. All you need is a little dirt, a little shovel and some coveralls. They sell them coveralls at K-Mart, don't they?"

"Stop hamming it up," Ellynne said.

Kenny pretended to be knocked out by her joke and rolled backwards, kicking sand on people and upsetting someone's tanning oil. Though Ellynne noticed that no one laughed, no one seemed very surprised or upset either. She guessed that Kenny was sort of the group clown. That surprised her in a way because he was so good-looking. But the funny thing about being around Kenny was that after a while, you sort of forgot he was as handsome as a movie star and related to his playful manner instead. Ellynne decided she liked him very much and was very glad she'd met him.

When he grabbed her hand, pulled her up off the towel and said, "Come on, I'll race you to the water," she went along eagerly. And when he called out, "Last one in's a loser," she spurted ahead of him, diving into the cold water. She was able to surface and call out to him, "That's you," before he swam away.

Four

The next few days fell into an easy pattern: she went to the beach every day about eleven o'clock and stayed there until it was time to go home and cook supper. Though there was a sameness about her life, Ellynne found that she was never bored.

She got to know a lot of people by sight and a few by name. Despite what she'd imagined, not everyone in the group made it to the beach every day and not everyone was accepted into the inner circle as easily as she was. Sailor, ChooChoo and Kenny were the focus of the group but Davy and two girls named Jenifer and Gloria were also there almost every day.

Some of the others were there a lot and there were always at least a dozen familiar faces each day when Ellynne arrived at the beach late in the morning. In a way, it was a lot like school because she quickly became a member of the inner circle and there were soon a lot of kids she didn't know saying hello to her. It gave her a sense of security to know that she'd been able to repeat her social success so readily. She genuinely enjoyed the kids she did talk with even though she spent most of her time with Kenny.

This crowd was a lot different from her friends at school, though. For one thing, they talked a lot less about the future and more about their immediate plans. Their conversation, like their lives, seemed to revolve around parties and the beach.

One morning, after she'd been coming to the beach for about a week, she arrived before Kenny did. She spread her towel beside Gloria and Jenifer, who made room for her and quickly began talking.

They joked and laughed about a television show they'd seen the night before and then the conversation drifted from television to movies. Soon, they were entertaining each other by trying to describe the worst movie they'd ever seen. *"Fast Times At Ridgemont High,"* Gloria said. "It had to be the worst. It was all about these weird surfers who drank all the time."

"Like Sailor," Jenifer said.

"Not like Sailor," Gloria answered in disgust. "At least that guy could stay on a board. Sailor's no surfer."

Ellynne was surprised by the comment but before she could find anything to say, the conversation took a lighter turn. Part of the reason Ellynne liked hanging out with this group so much was that everyone seemed to know how to enjoy life — something she was beginning to suspect was a valuable quality.

Abruptly, Gloria asked, "How's it going between you and Kenny?" Ellynne was a little surprised at the question and she answered cautiously, "We're just friends."

"Sure," Gloria said. "Kenny's good at being just friends."

"Don't pay any attention to her," Jenifer advised. "She's hard on all men this week."

"I wasn't being hard on Kenny," Gloria protested. "I was just being sympathetic."

"Does Kenny have a girlfriend?" Ellynne asked. She wasn't sure it was a good idea to talk about him when he wasn't there but she couldn't resist asking.

"Just you," Jenifer assured her.

"I meant besides me."

"No, and he really likes you, I can tell," Jenifer answered quickly.

"He's never asked me out," Ellynne admitted.

Jenifer and Gloria laughed at the idea and Jenifer explained. "Kenny doesn't go out unless you count partying."

"Oh." Ellynne didn't know what else to say so she switched the subject. "Do you come down here a lot in the winter too?"

"I do," Jenifer said. "At least I did last year. I was in school for an hour in the morning and I'd usually head down to the beach after that."

When she saw how perplexed Ellynne looked, she explained, "I flunked Senior English so I had to repeat it. I could have gone to summer school but I figured I might as well hang around for another year before I went to work."

"Will you find a job this fall?" Ellynne asked.

"Probably not," Jenifer admitted, "but I promised my mom I'd start to look." Then she laughed and said, "I figure I can get Christmas work and keep it till about Easter. That should make her happy."

Ellynne turned to Gloria and asked, "Will you look for work too?"

Gloria shrugged and ran her hands through the sand. "I thought I was getting married in the fall. My boyfriend's in the service, but now he says he wants to wait another year."

"That's why she's in such a rotten mood," Jenifer explained to Ellynne. "But I say at least he wants to marry you," she said to Gloria. "How many guys will do that these days?"

"Yeah," Gloria agreed, "even the nice ones like Kenny want to live at home till they're thirty and let their mothers take care of them."

"But Kenny's in school," Ellynne defended him.

Both girls laughed and Gloria said, "Is he?"

When Kenny got there that day he was full

of talk about getting his car fixed by a buddy of a neighbor. Ellynne listened for a while and then she asked, "Will you use the car to commute to school?"

Kenny didn't explain why he'd told her a lie, he just said, "Yeah, if I go."

"I thought you were a college student," Ellynne accused.

"I thought you were an orphan," he teased, "now I find out you're deserting me on July 4th for a family picnic."

"It's not my family picnic. My best friend's family is having it and I told Willie I would go months ago. Her folks planned this party in April when they put their pool in and finished decorating their backyard."

"I thought I was your best friend," Kenny pouted. "Party won't be the same without you."

"Yes it will," Ellynne teased. "I've never been to one of your parties."

"Yeah? Why not?"

"For one thing, you've never invited me."

Kenny laughed and said, "I'm inviting you now."

The next thing Ellynne knew he had jumped up and ran down to the water, diving into a huge wave.

F^{ive}

Ellynne was eager to show off her new tan to Willie, so she wore white shorts and a white sleeveless tee shirt with one large blue polka dot on the back and front. Red thongs and a red "just in case" nylon windbreaker completed her costume. She brushed her long hair into a smooth cascade of gold and noted with pleasure that the sun had lightened it even more than the bleach she'd applied last fall. When her mother suggested she wear something else, she said, "It's just a picnic." But when Willie opened the door and was wearing a light yellow sundress and high heeled shoes she was sorry she hadn't worn something more dressed up. Her mother, who had chosen a Hawaiian silk shirt and dressy pants, couldn't resist whispering in her ear, "I told you so."

Ellynne ignored her mother and said to

her beautiful friend, "You look great. Like the job is agreeing with you."

"I like it," Willie said, "but it's hard work. It took me a long time to clean the dirt out from under my nails for this party. And I sure am glad to be in a dress; I wear coveralls and hipboots most of the time."

The word "coveralls" reminded her of Kenny and she smiled. He would be at exactly the same spot on the beach today, doing exactly the same thing as usual. When she'd asked him if his folks had planned a celebration, he'd said, "I'm an orphan." Though she was getting to know him really well, she still didn't know much about him.

He almost never mentioned his family or what he did when he wasn't at the beach, but she had learned from the others that he lived in North Redondo with his mother. His mother had divorced his father, "when I was a puppy," Kenny had said and then he'd gone into an imitation of a puppy.

"I've got to play hostess for a while but I'm dying to talk to you. I have some questions." Willie raised her eyebrow and smiled at Ellynne as though they were about to swap secrets. She added, "I want to hear all about *him*."

"Him?" Judith Aleese asked.

"She means Kip," Ellynne said very quickly and Willie immediately fell in with her statement, nodding her head in agreement. "I've only talked to Kip on the phone twice," Ellynne said, feeling terrible about deceiving her mother but not wanting to get into explaining about Kenny. All Judith knew was that she had a group of friends she was meeting on the beach and Ellynne had been happy to let her believe the friends were from school.

"I miss Kip," Judith said. "Just when I got used to finding him there every time I came in from school, he disappeared." Then she laughed and said, "But I suppose he'll be back on my couch the day school starts. El Camino isn't very far away."

"Sure he will," Willie said and then she took Judith's arm and said, "I want you to meet my folks and some of the others. My mom's over there."

She led them through the livingroom to the sliding doors that led out to the backyard patio. Since Ellynne had been there many times, she was used to the elegant setting but she had a feeling that Judith was surprised, even though she'd told her about the Wilsons' house.

There really wasn't a backyard because it was all decks and swimming pool and the only plants were expensive container specimens. Judith said, "This is the kind of California house that they always show in the magazines but I've never actually been inside one before. It's beautiful."

"We had to make a choice," Willie's mother said, "either we had green grass or the pool. There just wasn't enough land for both. So we voted and I won."

"Who didn't want the pool?" Judith asked.

"Willie and her father," Mrs. Wilson said. "Actually, I think my husband was afraid he'd have to take care of it, and Willie wanted a garden, but since I'm the fastest talker, I won."

Mrs. Wilson did talk fast, emitting the same kind of attractive energy that Willie did as she circulated among her guests, introducing people, offering them another drink and generally making sure that the party kept moving. So many of Willie's mannerisms were like her mother's that it was amusing to watch the two of them together. They both held their heads slightly to one side when they talked and laughed, using their animated faces and active hands to emphasize a point. What made it doubly amusing was that Willie's mother was rather short and round while Willie was physically a carbon copy of her lean and taciturn father.

Dr. Wilson seemed very proud of his wife and daughter but he didn't talk much except to question his guests about how they wanted their steaks. Ellynne wondered if being a psychiatrist and having to listen to people's problems made him quiet, or if he was naturally that way.

While he watched the barbecuing steaks, Willie and her mother set out the other foods on a long, narrow table that was actually more like a redwood shelf against the tall redwood fence.

Ellynne offered to help them get the food ready but they both shook their heads, insisting that they could do it easier and faster because they knew their way around the kitchen.

"Go enjoy yourself," Mrs. Wilson said, and pushed Ellynne into a crowd of adults who were having a serious discussion about the environment. Ellynne stood in the circle, holding her Coke, letting her mind wander as she half-listened to one woman talking about what was going on along the California seashore.

Most of the time, Ellynne was busy looking around the party at the other guests. There were about twenty people and she was the only person Willie's age, something that she'd been prepared for when she was invited. Most of the guests were somewhere around the Dr. and Mrs. Wilson's age — about forty — but a few of them were older and younger than that.

The woman who was talking must be in her sixties, Ellynne decided, and she wasn't one of those made-up, youngish sixty-year-olds that you saw so many of in California, either. This woman had her gray hair whacked off in a haircut not too different from ChooChoo's punk cut. She was wearing a Mexican cotton dress she'd probably bought on a trip about twenty years ago. What amused Ellynne the most was that she was wearing suede sandals from Germany that some of the kids she knew really thought were the most "in" thing they could have. They were the kind of shoes you bought in health food stores and funky little places. As Ellynne looked at this woman she found herself getting caught up in what she was saying about the environmental problems that California was facing.

". . . the pelicans almost died twice," she was saying, "once because of the DDT and then because of those crazy fishermen cutting off their beaks. And now it's the whales we're losing."

"And what about the dolphins? They get caught in the nets of the tuna fishermen and drown because they can't get up out of the water for air. Can you imagine a world without dolphins? We've got to find the people power to mobilize before it's too late. If this new bill passes, the Environmental Protection Agency will really be a joke; they'll eventually kill off all the sea life."

"It's not just the sea life," another woman said. "The beaches are filthy these days. I took my three-year-old swimming last week and he cut his foot on a piece of broken glass. Beer cans all around — it's a disgrace!"

Ellynne had to agree with what the woman said about the beaches being dirty. She hated to see trash and cans lying around spoiling the natural beauty. She might have added something to the conversation but Willie approached the group.

"Come on," Willie tugged Ellynne's elbow,

"I want to hear all about your summer romance."

"What summer romance?" Ellynne answered, as she allowed herself to be led away from the group and into the corner of the patio where they perched on the edge of a giant redwood tub that held a twenty-foot olive tree.

"Have you told Kip?" Willie wanted to know.

"There's absolutely nothing to tell," Ellynne protested. "I made a friend at the beach, that's all. He's just a friend."

Willie dropped her head to one side quizzically, as though she was trying to decide if Ellynne was hiding something. Finally she said, "This friend is movie star handsome. You said so yourself. He's twenty years old and you're spending all day, every day with him, but he's just a friend. Do you think I should believe that?"

Ellynne shrugged. "It's hard to explain but he *is* just a friend and he *is* movie star handsome. He's not twenty though, just nineteen." She'd learned Kenny's real age from Sailor, who'd boasted that he was almost old enough to buy liquor legally but Kenny had two years to go. She didn't add that she'd also learned that Kenny wasn't really enrolled in college yet but planned to go in the fall.

"Has he asked you out yet?"

Ellynne shook her head. "He isn't exactly like that. I mean, I'm not sure Kenny ever asks anyone out. Besides, I told him about Kip."

"You told him about Kip but you haven't told Kip about him. What does it signify?" Willie bent over and waved her long, slender fingers over an imaginary crystal ball. Affecting a fake Gypsy accent, she said, "Madame Willie sees trouble and confusion ahead. What's this? A tall, dark man and a tall, blond man, and a beautiful girl in the middle. A beautiful girl with an unclear head and a murky heart."

Ellynne laughed heartily and said, "That's the way Kenny is. He jokes around a lot. He's fun but no one to be serious about."

"Then why haven't you told Kip?" Willie teased.

"I've only talked to Kip twice since he took that job, and, I've already told you, I'm not serious about Kenny."

"O.K. Don't be mad at me. You haven't seen me or talked to me more than twice either but you *did* tell me about Kenny. In fact, that's mostly what you talked about."

"It's hard when people ask you what you've been doing and you haven't been doing anything. What was I supposed to answer? Jelling?"

"Jelling?"

"You know, relaxing totally."

"I know." Willie's voice had a tinge of disapproval as she asked, "Since when do you use words like 'jell?' "

"I use all kinds of words."

"Surfing words. It seems to me that for someone who's of absolutely no importance to you at all, this Kenny's really influencing you. You're dressing like a surfer, using surfing words."

"There are all kinds of surfers. I'd think you, of all people, wouldn't stereotype people."

"Because I'm black?"

"Because you're a cheerleader."

Both girls seemed to realize they were dangerously close to quarreling so they quickly changed the subject to Willie's job. In a few minutes, Ellynne was completely relaxed, laughing at Willie's stories about her adventures with the nursery plants and her simple chores. ". . . So she said if you spray plants they'll get rusty, and I thought it had something to do with the tin cans they were in but it turned out it meant spotted leaves. You have to learn a new vocabulary even to walk around in hip boots and heft tin cans around," Willie explained.

"It's the same in everything," Ellynne said. "I was listening to your mom's friend talk about the environmental problems of the seashore and she used so many technical words that she lost me and most of the others."

"Vicky? She's sort of my adopted grandmother, except she's moved to San Diego now. Her husband was my dad's partner but now that she's a widow Vicky spends all her time volunteering at Sea World. Remember when those crazy fishermen were cutting off the beaks of pelicans so they couldn't catch fish? Well Vicky read about it in the newspaper and volunteered her services. I don't know if she actually helped put the fiberglass beaks on the birds or if she helped out in some other way but she got hooked on the subject of environmental problems on the beaches. She's worked at it practically full-time ever since. Now she wants me to be an oceanographer."

Willie took a deep breath and continued. "Actually, I'm thinking of taking some marine biology courses during my freshman year. I still think I want a science career, but one thing this job's taught me is that I really don't want to be a horticulturist. I don't care what they say about how talking to plants is good for them and how they respond and all that, they never talk back. At least working with porpoises would be interesting. Did you know they're trying to teach them to talk?"

"Even if they learn, they won't get a word in edgewise when they're around you," Ellynne teased.

"It's hard to know what you want to do," Willie complained.

"Kip thinks he was mostly interested in science because Mr. Morales was such a good teacher," Ellynne said. "But he's going to try and take some business courses at El Camino as well as science."

"That's a good idea," Willie said. "It's really easy to figure out what you *don't* want, but there are so many choices. My mom says when she got out of college women basically had fewer choices."

"At least you know you want science," Ellynne said. "All I know is I want an Ivy League school and I'm not even sure that's my ambition or my mother's."

"Any chance of early admission?" Willie asked. Both girls had applied for early admission to several schools and Willie already had hers from Davis.

"No. Besides, I have to get a 4.0 next year if I'm going to get a scholarship. It will bring my 3.6 up to a 3.7 and then there might be a chance. Without the scholarship, I'm in trouble."

They spent more time talking about their college and career plans until Mr. Wilson announced that it was time to eat. Ellynne joined her mother and three others at one of the small card tables that were set up for eating.

After lunch, Ellynne made a point to help Mrs. Wilson with the cleanup, claiming that she had a special right to on account of her age. Then everyone went upstairs to the Wilsons' deck where they had a great view of the fireworks that were being set off on the beach.

The Wilson bedroom was larger than the livingroom of the apartment that Ellynne and her mother shared and, like the rest of the house, it was furnished in striking modern decor. They had brought chairs up from the lower floor and formed a sort of theater with rows of seats because the fireworks display lasted almost two hours.

During the fireworks, Ellynne helped Willie pour drinks for people and they were kept so busy that they really didn't have time to talk anymore. As they said good-bye Ellynne said, "I really miss you. When's your next day off?"

"Christmas," Willie joked. Then she added, "I'm getting used to the schedule so maybe I'll feel up to doing something one night. We could eat pizza and go to the early show. But five a.m. comes awful early so it has to be the early show."

"Call me anytime next week," Ellynne said.

"You won't be busy?" Willie asked. "Kip not coming home?"

"He's on the same schedule you are only at Disneyland," Ellynne answered. "But while you guys work like little demons, I'm thinking of you. Feeling guilty and all that."

Willie laughed and said, "*You're* the demon, rubbing it in. But you just remember that hard work pays off."

"In rough hands and bent backs," Ellynne answered. It was one of Kenny's lines but she didn't bother telling Willie that. There had been enough talk about Kenny already that evening.

On the way home from the party, her mother sighed and said, "I'm glad I got to see inside a house like that. It gives me something to aspire to, but I'm afraid that lawyers don't earn as much as psychiatrists. We'll never be able to afford anything that fancy. Besides, you'll soon be gone to college and that will take just about everything we have put away. You know, when your father died the money he left seemed like plenty, but my college and yours will not only take every penny, I'll probably end up in debt. Be worth it though. A good education is foundation for life. That's what my mother always said."

"Maybe I'll get a scholarship," Ellynne said. "Maybe you won't have to spend so much." She didn't even bother to suggest that she might do as Kip was doing and spend a year in El Camino Junior College because she knew her mother would never settle for that sort of beginning. Besides, her situation was a lot different from Kip's. He would really have to save every penny he could and borrow the rest to make it through California schools.

"I'm sure you could get a scholarship somewhere," her mother answered, "but you're going to the best. I want the best for you, Ellynne."

"Maybe I'll get a scholarship to Yale," Ellynne said. "My counselor said I had a chance since Dad went there."

"Princeton, Yale, it doesn't matter. What matters is to make it into one of them. We'll find the money." Judith let her arm rest on Ellynne's shoulder for a moment and switched the subject. "Willie's mother was fun, just like Willie is. I told her we'd have them over sometime this summer. Think you'd like to cook the meal?"

"Sure." Ellynne's mind raced as she ran through her collection of recipes searching for something she felt was possible to serve to Dr. and Mrs. Wilson. Could you do roast hot dogs under glass?

"I signed up for Vicky Greenbaum's Save The Beaches campaign. And I told her you'd help organize the high school. You and Willie."

"Mother, why did you do that?"

"I assumed you'd be interested. You seem to love the beach so much."

Ellynne didn't really think her mother had the right to volunteer her services that way, but she was determined not to fight with her mother that evening, so she said, "I do."

"Then you can donate a few hours a week to the cause," her mother said. "You certainly have plenty of time."

"The fireworks were nice, weren't they?" Ellynne asked, changing the subject.

"So was the party. What did you and Willie talk about for so long? It sounded like it was very funny."

Ellynne entertained her mother with Willie's stories as they drove into their garage and climbed the stairs to their apartment. Once inside, her mother stretched and yawned and said, "That was the most fun I've had all summer. One of these days I'm going to give a party myself. Maybe invite all the people from school. One of these days when I get more energy. I think I almost envy you your summer off, Ellynne. Are you still enjoying it?"

"Love it."

"Good," her mother said and kissed her on the forehead. "I want you to be happy. You're only young once." Then she turned to go to her bedroom, leaving Ellynne to turn off the lights and lock up.

S^{ix}

Ellynne studied harder the next morning than anytime since summer vacation started, partly because her conversation with Willie had brought her long term goals closer to the forefront of her mind, and partly because she realized that getting a scholarship would really take a big financial burden off her mother.

Her original plan had been to read all of the novels and short stories that would be required in Senior English during the vacation so she would have more time to spend on her other work. Since they hadn't changed the curriculum in fifteen years, she was betting they wouldn't this year either. Even if they did change one of the novels, she reasoned, she would have completed the others in advance. There was no way they were going to prepare new study guides and tests for all six novels or the two short story anthologies.

When she'd devised the plan, it had seemed like the most painless thing she could do to get ahead of the senior year scholastics. But now that three weeks of summer vacation were gone and she was still on page six of the first novel, she could see that the plan was going to need some revision.

"Dreams can come true," she reminded herself. In the past, hard work had paid off for her and there was no reason to believe that it wouldn't this time. Yet a small voice inside her whispered, "What's the use? Even if you do get straight A's next year, there's no guarantee you'll get a scholarship. Just like there was no guarantee that you'd get the place on the cheerleading team."

Despite her discouragement, she slugged her way through the first fifty pages of *The Magic Mountain*. She then took the slimmest book, the only one that was paperback, and wrapped it up in her towel to take to the beach. Maybe she would be able to have her cake and eat it too, she told herself, and closed her study session at 12:30.

Before she left the apartment, she took some hamburger out of the freezer to thaw. After yesterday's feast at the Wilsons', she figured her mother wouldn't complain about simple food tonight. Anyway, there were some fresh strawberries that she could serve with ice cream to dress things up a bit.

As she walked toward Kenny and his friends, she thought about her conversation with Willie the night before, going over it in her own mind to decide whether she had been telling Willie the whole truth about her friendship with Kenny. It was true she'd known him for more than two weeks and they had never done anything together except go to the beach, but it wasn't exactly true that nothing at all romantic was going on between them.

Kenny held her hand a lot, usually when they walked on the sand or ran into the ocean. She was also aware that he liked to touch her when they talked. Lately, he'd found excuses to play games with her that were more physical than just his ordinary jokes. Though he'd never said anything more about her being his girlfriend, the other kids treated her as though she was.

For that matter, she knew she hadn't been entirely honest about not mentioning Kenny to Kip because it didn't seem important to her. Kip and she *had* only talked twice and both times it had been mostly about Kip's job. He had originally been hired as a sweeper and was delighted because he'd quickly been promoted to one of the attendants on the docks of the jungle ride. The last time he'd called, they'd talked mostly about the possibility that he might be admitted to an executive training program at Disneyland. He said they looked for "real winners." The program even offered college scholarships to students who would make a commitment to working at Disneyland when they graduated.

"Of course it would mean a career in business, not science," Kip had said. He'd waited, obviously asking for her reaction.

"I'm sure you'll be picked, Kip," Ellynne had said.

"Maybe," he'd said. "We can worry about that when it happens, right?"

Ellynne was being careful to keep the conversation centered around his work, not around her summer. *I'm a coward,* she thought. Even when he'd asked her if she was tired of loafing yet, she'd just said that she was a little bored. *But I'm not bored,* she admitted to herself. *I'm loving every minute of it.*

Still, telling a little fib about her mood wasn't an important lie and nothing had really happened between her and Kenny at all. So why was she feeling so guilty? Ellynne didn't like to admit it, even to herself, but she really had hidden things from Kip, just as Willie had suggested. That's why she felt so defensive with Willie and so guilty now.

She decided the next time Kip called her she would casually work Kenny's name into the conversation. She couldn't call him because he was working such long hours and he was also signing up to substitute for others who missed work. Kip wanted to earn as much as possible this summer and he was putting it all away for college expenses.

Ellynne admired the fact that Willie and Kip were working so hard. Remembering her conversation with her mother last night, she felt a little guilty that she had been so stubborn about not looking for a job herself. Even though she was only fifteen, she might have found something. *If I use the summer to get a scholarship, it will be worth more than a job would be,* Ellynne told herself. But that same small voice which had earlier told her hard work might not pay off now whispered, "But you really aren't using the summer for studying, are you?"

Thoughts of school and future plans clouded her mind so completely that she really didn't enjoy the walk the way she usually did.

Now she lifted her head and looked out at the ocean, pausing to really see the deep greens and blues that made patches on the glossy surface of the water. There were no surfers because they were only allowed to use the beach until nine in the morning, but farther out there she could see several white sails. Even though it was the day after a holiday, she was surprised to see how many sailboats there were and how close to shore they sailed. She wasn't the only one who enjoyed leisure time, she told herself.

There were lots more sailboats a little farther south, toward the Palos Verdes cape, and to Ellynne they looked like small little birds bobbing on the ocean; she thought they were beautiful and promised herself that one day she would go sailing. Maybe Kenny would take her. He seemed to want to take her places and introduce her to new experiences. He kept saying he'd take her to San Clemente as soon as he got his car fixed to see a friend of his who owned a surf shop on that beach. He'd also promised to take her up to Santa Barbara sometime this summer. But the voice inside her head wouldn't quit spouting discouraging words. It asked her the question, "But where has he taken you so far? Out for a Coke?"

She had to admit that Kenny didn't even buy her a Coke very often. In fact, she was usually the one with the money to throw into the pot when someone went for a "food raid" to the local store.

As she worried over all these discouraging facts, she stepped into something slimy and jumped back, fully expecting it to be a jelly fish. Those poisonous creatures that looked like a cross between a wet baggie from the kitchen and an improbable monster from a Spielberg movie sometimes drifted up onto the beach. Though Ellynne had only seen a couple from a safe distance, she knew that stepping on one could be dangerous. In fact, she'd heard of one surfer who'd gotten caught in a whole school of them off the end of the pier and ended up in the hospital because of the poisonous stings.

But she hadn't stepped on a jelly fish, just a messy peanut butter and jelly sandwich that someone had apparently abandoned. Now it was either washed up on the water's edge from some other place, or the high tide had claimed it from the sand. Ellynne shuddered and washed the mess off her foot in the surf.

The mashed sandwich was falling out of its wrapping paper. Close beside it was a water-logged box of cookies. She thought about picking all the garbage up and decided it would be too gross an activity to add to an already gross day. Feeling guilty, she left the abandoned lunch to its fate.

When she got to the place where Kenny and his friends were, there was no room for her towel next to his. In fact, he was almost completely surrounded by other people, almost as though he were the center of a cluster of beach towels. He was lying on his back, with his eyes shut.

"Hi," Ellynne said, in her loudest voice.

Several people said hello to her but Kenny didn't open his eyes. She wondered for a minute if he was asleep but decided he wasn't, though she wasn't sure how she knew exactly. Sailor said, "He had a hard night," as though in explanation. "You should have been there to pick up the pieces."

There it was again, that assumption that she and Kenny were seeing each other in the evenings, when the truth was that he'd never even asked her for her telephone number or her last name. She spread out her towel on the only bare patch of sand close to the group and tried not to let it bother her that Kenny was quite obviously ignoring her. "Where did you go?" she asked Sailor.

"Go?" Sailor asked. "You mean last night? Here. We had a party here."

"Weren't there a lot of police around?"

"Cops were too busy to worry about it," Sailor said. Then he grinned, sat down on his haunches and reached into a paper bag beside him, picked out a beer and pulled the tab. "Want one?" he asked.

"No," she said firmly. Ellynne knew he'd think she was square or childish or something but she didn't care. Either this crowd wasn't the only group that partied here last night or they'd had an awful lot because she could see that the beach was littered with beer and soda cans.

But Sailor didn't seem to take offense, he just nodded and drank deeply from the can. "They used to really patrol at nights but they don't have as much money now so they don't have the manpower to do the job. You can party here just about anytime now. Not like the old days when they'd run you in. In a way, it kind of spoils the fun, but it keeps things cool, the way we like them." Sailor grinned and crunched the can with one practiced motion. He raised his arm to throw it away.

"Don't throw that," Ellynne said sharply.

"Lots of others."

"Why would you want to litter the beach you love?" she asked. She could hear that her voice contained a mixture of curiosity and contempt but she genuinely didn't care if she made him angry.

Sailor didn't answer and Kenny opened his eyes, apparently curious enough about what was going on to admit he was awake.

Ellynne said, "I should think you'd want to keep this beach beautiful, especially since it's practically your home."

Sailor looked bored and turned away. Kenny sat up, grinned and said, "One day with your family and you sound just like them. What did you do, eat patriotic pie?"

"I just don't want the beach to get messed up," Ellynne answered. "I just think it's a crime to use something and waste it."

"Wasted," Sailor interrupted. "Let's get wasted. Anybody got any more beer money?"

There was a silence and Sailor, seeing his idea was meeting with no approval, grinned and said, "Guess I'll see if I can get some shuteye." With that, he turned and lay face down on his towel. The three other people who had been watching the scene between Ellynne and Sailor, seeing that there would be no further fireworks, got up and walked toward the water. ChooChoo, who was the only other person there, had never even lifted her head so Ellynne wasn't sure whether she really was awake or asleep.

"Patriotic pie, that's what they fed my girl. Made her a regular little soldier too. Look at that fire in her eyes."

"You too," Ellynne blazed again. "I should think you'd care what happens to your home too."

He put his hands on his waist and asked, "Am I to assume, Madame, that you are suggesting that I am a homeless beach bum? My dear Madame, I'll have you know that I once had a house that was a regular palace with diamonds for dinner and crushed rubies for drink but I threw it all away for love. Fell in love with a spitfire and she. . . ."

"Forget it," Ellynne broke in, trying not to laugh and knowing that Kenny had charmed her out of her mood. "I'll pick up the beer cans myself."

"I'll help you," Kenny said and jumped up, then began hopping up and down like a monkey, chattering and scratching under his arms.

Ellynne was really laughing as she turned from him and started collecting beer cans and carrying them toward the trash can at the foot of the stairs leading to the beach. At first, she was making the long trip across the sand for every two cans and then she figured out that she could carry six at a time if she stuck her fingers in the holes just right. When she did that, Kenny pretended to be really excited and hopped along behind her with his six cans.

Eventually, they cleaned up all the cans in their area and Ellynne felt a lot better as she sat down on her towel. Kenny who had hopped until the very end, turned into himself again when she sat down and asked, "Why are you way over there?"

"No room next to you."

"We'll move Sailor."

"It's not important."

"To you, maybe," Kenny said, "but it's very important to me. Can't have me and my girl separated by a slug from the depths of the sea." He stood over Sailor and nudged his inert body as though he were trying to scoot him over. At first, Sailor tried to ignore him, but eventually he got up and spread his towel out on the other side of ChooChoo, leaving room for Ellynne next to Kenny.

During all this, ChooChoo never moved a muscle and Ellynne wondered what, if anything, the beautiful girl really thought about all the actions taking place around her. She was on the beach every day, and so far Ellynne had counted that she had eight different bathing suits, but she never went in the water and she never talked unless she was more or less forced to. Ellynne was sure that she could spend the rest of her life next to this girl on the beach and never learn a thing about her.

Of all the people there, ChooChoo was the biggest mystery to Ellynne and yet, she couldn't help but admire the way the girl looked and the daring sorts of clothing she wore. Just dying your hair bright blonde and then shearing it all off took tremendous courage, so she must be an interesting person, Ellynne reasoned, though she'd never seen any signs of it. She decided that she and ChooChoo just didn't have anything in common.

That small voice that had been so troublesome all morning asked her, *What do you really have in common with any of them?*

Seven

When Kenny kissed her the first time, Ellynne was amazed at how natural it felt. They were holding hands and walking along the edge of the beach at the end of a long day. Since her mother had a late class, Ellynne had let the afternoon drift into evening. She and Kenny swam, talked a bit, and mostly just lay on the sand enjoying the warm sunshine.

About six p.m., Ellynne stood up and said, "Guess I'd better go."

"What's the hurry?"

"I'm hungry and kind of sleepy," Ellynne admitted. It never ceased to amaze her how tired lying on the beach made her. Though she loved every minute of it, the sun seemed to just pull energy out of her, turning her into a rag doll on sand.

"Let's take a walk," Kenny said. "Then we can get some burgers. O.K.?"

Surprised by the invitation, Ellynne nodded her head. It was now three weeks since she'd met Kenny and this was the first actual invitation he'd offered. He took her by the hand and they walked down to the water's edge and then turned toward the Palos Verdes cape. Walking silently, with the dark red sun on her right side and Kenny on her left, Ellynne felt totally relaxed and happy. It was a feeling she'd looked for all her life.

She saw a movement out on the water and paused, holding her hand to her forehead to block out some of the sun's strong light, so she could make out what was happening more clearly. She said, "There's something moving out there. A lot of them."

"If it's fins, don't tell me. I scare easy."

"Not fins," Ellynne answered. "Sort of jumping lumps. Could it be whales?"

"Where?"

Ellynne pointed out to sea and as she pointed, she realized that whatever it was was moving closer to the shore. "I wish I had some opera glasses," she said. Then she laughed. "Opera glasses and a bikini — what a costume. Are they whales?"

"Dolphins," Kenny answered. "And they're coming closer. They come in really close sometimes."

"Looking for fish?"

"Just to play," Kenny answered. "They're not like other fish."

"They're not fish," Ellynne said.

"Yeah, but they're sort of like fish," Kenny argued.

It was no time for a science lesson and she was much too enthralled by the sight in front of her anyway. By now, the leaping dolphins were close to the shore, just about twenty feet out from where the waves broke and she could make out that there were several of them — possibly six. They seemed to be full of energy as they jumped up out of the water, forming a sort of circular missile of themselves as they dove back in.

She and Kenny stood silently at the water's edge for several minutes, holding hands and watching the dolphins play. For Ellynne, it was one of the most exciting things she had ever seen and she felt almost like crying when they swam away. She asked, "Have you seen them before?"

"Once," Kenny answered. "But I've seen lots of whales. They migrate through here and you can see them off the end of the pier or on your board if you're lucky."

"You can also take a boat," Ellynne said.

"If you've got the money," Kenny agreed. Then he turned slightly and took her other hand in his, pulling her toward him. He did not put his arms around her but she felt so close to him that she could almost hear his heart beating as he bent his head and kissed her. The kiss was sweet and long and Ellynne responded easily as their lips blended together.

Finally, he dropped her hands and she pulled back slightly, almost dizzy from the impact of the kiss. For the first time, she understood completely why she'd been so interested in being friendly with Kenny. It wasn't just a friendship at all. It was a different kind of romance, one that was natural, easy and relaxed. Not that she hadn't felt relaxed with Kip, but. . . .

Kenny was smiling at her now and his light blue eyes seemed to give off a blaze of warmth as he said, "Didn't I tell you you were my girl?"

He's beautiful, Ellynne thought. It seemed like a funny word to use to describe a boy, but Kenny was so handsome that he really seemed almost beautiful to her. His pale blonde hair was almost golden in the deepening reds of the sunset and his skin was radiating gold. She said aloud, "You know what you are? You're a golden boy. Ever hear that expression?"

He dropped his head to one side, stuck a finger in his mouth, assuming his shy, hayseed farmer personality and said, "Cain't say that I ever have, Ma'am."

"It means someone who's really lucky," Ellynne said. "Someone who the sun always shines on, no matter if it's raining outside. Someone special."

"Then you must be my sunshine," he answered in that funny hillbilly drawl. Then he began to sing at the top of his voice, "You are my sunshine/My only sunshine. . . ."

Ellynne stuck her fingers in her ears and ran back toward their spot on the beach. Kenny caught up with her easily, grabbing her around the waist, and they ran in tandem with their arms around each other. When they got back to their towels, everyone else was gone. Ellynne bent over to pick up her towel and began shaking it, then folding it and rolling it into a small bundle.

Kenny was standing beside her, watching her movements and he said in an admiring voice, "You're so neat. How did you get so neat?"

Ellynne shook her head. "I'm not so neat."

"Sure you are. Picking up beer cans in your spare time, rolling up towels. You even mark your place in that book with a paper napkin."

"Why not?" Ellynne couldn't tell whether his observations were criticism or not and she was amazed to discover how much she cared.

"Most people would just toss the book down, or I guess a lot would have tossed it away."

"I need to study," she knew her voice sounded defensive but she'd already explained it to Kenny more than once. He seemed to take her studies as a kind of joke. "There's nothing funny about studying, you know."

"What will it get you?" Kenny asked.

"A scholarship, if I'm lucky," Ellynne answered. "Where are we going for burgers?"

"Got any money?"

"Three dollars."

"Better go to McDonalds," Kenny answered. "Unless you want to make them."

Ellynne thought it over. She didn't really have any sort of agreement with Judith about bringing friends home, though she had a feeling that her mother might not be crazy about the idea. Still, she was a senior in high school. So how could her mother really object to her having Kenny over for supper?

"Good idea," Ellynne said, trying to keep things as casual and natural as Kenny did. He didn't seem to think there was anything momentous about their first kiss or the fact that he'd actually suggested doing something together in the evening but to her, the whole world seemed changed.

That evening, he seemed to enjoy sitting on her couch and watching TV after they'd eaten. During the commercials they kissed, and once Ellynne tried to start a serious conversation, saying, "I don't know if I think Sailor's such a good influence on you."

"Sailor? We go way back."

"He drinks a lot."

"Yeah, but I don't. You going to turn into one of those bossy women now that we're going together?" He was smiling when he asked the question but Ellynne had the feeling it was a serious one; his light blue eyes were steady as he waited for her answer.

"I just hate the way some kids seem to throw their lives away on liquor before they're even old enough to drink. It's ridiculous."

"How about popcorn?" he asked. "Got anything against popcorn?"

"Be serious."

"I am serious. I'm a popcornaholic. Actually get these withdrawal symptoms when I don't get my popcorn fix. I begin to twitch and then I see things . . ." He held his hands up over his eyes and called out, "Oh no . . . go away monsters . . . I've got no popcorn for you."

Ellynne was laughing as she went to the kitchen to make the popcorn.

"It's hard to explain," she said to Willie as they ate pizza in the mall. They were going to the early movie and Ellynne had just confessed that her relationship with Kenny had totally changed. "You'd think I'd feel guilty or something, but all I feel is natural when he kisses me. Natural, only it's really wonderful. It's hard to explain. . . ."

"I don't see anything very difficult about it," Willie said. "You're obviously involved in a red hot summer romance. When school starts, you may change your mind."

"But I'm not sure I will," Ellynne said. "Anyway, I think I should break up with Kip."

"Break up? Don't you think that's a little drastic? You've been crazy about Kip ever since you met him and you two get along so well. Nothing you've told me about Kenny makes me think you feel that crazy about him."

"But I do," Ellynne said. "Only it's hard to explain. . . ."

"You mentioned that," Willie teased. "When do I get to meet Mr. Unexplainable?"

"I'm not sure." Why was she so reluctant to introduce Kenny to Willie and her other friends? She certainly didn't think it was that she was ashamed of him. More like she wanted to keep her summer experience private and special. Bringing Kenny into her everyday world might diminish the magic.

"Bring him to the nursery one day," Willie said. "I'm dying to get a look at him at least."

"As soon as he gets his car fixed," Ellynne promised. "Right now all he has is a bicycle."

"Well, you could ride the bus or maybe even walk," Willie said. "The exercise might do you good."

"What does that mean?"

"Means you look like you might have put on a pound or two in the wrong places."

Ellynne shoved the pizza plate away from her and said, "That's part of what I'm talking about. I worked so hard to get that thirty pounds off and now I have to work to not gain weight. You never gain, no matter what, but I'll probably always have to struggle with it. And then the cheerleading thing — I worked so hard and didn't even get it."

Willie raised one eyebrow and asked, "Is this Ellynne or Kenny talking?"

"Why do you keep harping on what a bad

influence he is on me?" Ellynne asked. "I was just trying to explain what I meant when I said I'm tired of trying so hard."

"O.K., Sweetie," Willie said soothingly. "I'm sorry I said you'd gained weight and I can see why you might still be a little bit disappointed about losing the cheerleader competition. I can even see why you want to date other guys. We've got no quarrel, Ellynne. I just want you to be happy. I want the best for you."

Ellynne's mood lifted and she laughed merrily. "That's what my mother always says to me, but the trouble is she's so darn sure that she knows exactly what the best should be. Sometimes I feel like asking, 'What if I'd just as soon have the second best? What if that is more fun?'"

Willie pushed her pizza away too and said, "You know, I may understand what you're saying better than you think. We're both only children who get a lot of pressure. For me, it may be even worse because I'm black. My folks are ambitious for me, too, and sometimes I catch my mom or my dad looking at me and there's so much love and pride there I just feel like panicking. I mean, when your parents expect so much and love you so much, you lay a lot on the line. Know what I mean?"

Ellynne smiled at her friend gratefully, knowing that she was understood and accepted. She said, "We are both pretty lucky and I guess in some ways that makes it harder."

"Not harder," Willie corrected. "But maybe more complicated. I don't always know if I'm doing something because my mom wants it or my dad wants it or I want it."

"The thing I liked best about going out for cheerleader was that it was all mine," Ellynne admitted. "I sure knew who wanted that and it wasn't my mother."

They were still laughing as they left the pizza parlor and went toward the movie. Before they went in, Ellynne promised, "I'll bring him by tomorrow for sure."

Eight

Kenny asked Gloria to drive Ellynne to the nursery so they could visit Willie. She didn't seem exactly crazy about the idea when Kenny brought it up and Ellynne wished he hadn't asked her. But when Gloria picked up her towel and took out her car keys, saying, "Come on," Ellynne had no choice but to follow. Kenny followed them on his bicycle so she would have someone to ride back with.

As they drove away, Ellynne said, "I really appreciate this."

"No problem," Gloria said. "It's on my way home anyway."

"You're leaving early," Ellynne said.

"Date tonight," Gloria explained. "I decided if he didn't want to marry me, I'd start looking around. So I'm going dancing with a friend of Davy's. You and Kenny want to come?"

"I'll ask him," Ellynne answered, trying to

behave as though it was as normal as apple pie to go dancing with Kenny. The truth of the matter was that they'd still never gone anywhere except to her house a few times when her mother had a late class.

When they pulled up in front of the nursery, Gloria turned off the ignition and waited for Kenny to catch up. He was only a couple of minutes behind them and when he got close enough, Gloria asked, "You and Ellynne want to go dancing tonight?"

"No bread."

Ellynne almost offered to pay but she remembered that she was just about out of money herself and she had a week to go before she got her check. If she was going to be able to pitch into the community collection for food, she would have to hold onto her last few dollars. She said, "Thanks for asking," to Gloria and got out of the car.

Ellynne enjoyed looking around the nursery and it gave her extra pleasure to know that her friend was responsible for the care of the thousands of plants that sat on benches, on gravel pits and plain dirt. The nursery was a big one, covering almost an acre of ground, and it took some time to find Willie, who turned out to be at the back of the nursery watering hundreds of begonias in tiny tin cans.

Willie was wearing huge men's coveralls and yellow hip boots plus a funny straw hat that Ellynne noticed she had tipped at a very stylish angle. When she saw them, she wiped her muddy hands on her muddy coveralls and put the hose down, saying, "Hi, Kenny, I really am glad to meet you. I hear so much about you from Ellynne."

"You too," Kenny said. He smiled at Willie and asked, "You in charge of all of this?"

"Not quite," Willie said. "But I am in charge of the lath house, beginning today. I got a promotion and a raise."

"That's wonderful," Ellynne said. It occurred to her that both Kip and Willie had done very well on their jobs this summer and that they would both be earning more than they'd originally planned.

The three of them walked through the open fields toward the lath house as Willie explained, "The plants in the lath house are especially difficult because they need exactly the right mixture of sun and shade. Of course the slatted roof provides that to a certain extent, but they also have to be checked twice a day for signs of browning or drowning."

"Browning and drowning," Kenny said, "that sounds like what my girl and me have been doing. Right?" He hugged Ellynne close and she smiled at him, but she found herself hoping that he wouldn't crack too many jokes around Willie. Willie ignored him and kept right on talking about her job and the plants. Ellynne interrupted once to ask, "Can plants really drown?"

"Sure they can. If their roots can't get oxygen, they go under."

"Like surfers," Kenny said. "Gloria got a

letter from Davy yesterday. I guess he almost drowned. Met some other guy at the section and went into the washing machine. By the time he was up, another bowl crashed on him. Poor old Davy, we almost lost him."

Willie said nothing but she stopped talking about her nursery job. Ellynne jumped into the conversation and said, "Davy is one of our beach friends and he's in Hawaii this week."

"Going to stay another week," Kenny said. He hugged Ellynne close to him again and said, "That's what Ellynne and I are saving our money for — a trip to the island."

Willie stared coolly at Kenny as she said, "That will be nice and I'm sure Judith will be overjoyed."

"Judith is my mother," Ellynne explained to Kenny.

"Ah yes, the fabulous Judith of the legal knowledge. I'm going to have to meet her soon."

"Yes," Ellynne said. Somehow, she had an idea that the meeting would go even worse than this one was. She had been right to want to keep Kenny and Willie apart. She felt terrible about the way the two of them obviously weren't hitting it off. Ellynne decided to try one more time. She said, "Willie's going to be an oceanographer."

"Maybe," Willie said.

"Then you can study me," Kenny beamed as he said it and Ellynne prayed that he wouldn't do one of his funny faces or voices.

She'd never known Willie to be so stiff and formal before and she guessed it was partly because her friend was working in a real job. But it was also because Kenny didn't seem to be trying very hard to communicate on her level.

"You can put me on your endangered species list," Kenny added. "Fellows like me are hard to find."

"I'm sure they are," Willie said dryly and Ellynne wished the afternoon had never happened.

"You've got to be kidding," Willie said when she called that evening.

Ellynne's temper flared and she asked, "Why?"

"He's not even a tenth as nice as Kip," Willie said. "He's handsome, I'll admit that, but he's a real lightweight in the brain department."

"No he's not," Ellynne said quickly. "He's really very bright and very nice. It's just that I think he was sort of out of his element and a little nervous."

"Are you planning to spend your whole life together on the beach? Getting married in your polka dot bikini?"

"Don't be sarcastic. We're not getting married, we're just sort of . . . going together."

"Sounded like his idea of going together went pretty far."

"What are you talking about? He's really

very — he's not pushy at all in that way."

"What about that trip to Hawaii?"

"Oh, that's just a dream of his. It will never happen."

"Why not?"

"Because he doesn't have any money. Because I have to go back to school in the fall. Because it just won't happen." She didn't tell Willie that she couldn't even get Kenny to take her dancing, let alone to Hawaii.

"And you're sure he's not dangerous?"

Ellynne laughed at the idea. "Kenny? He's a real sweet guy. No problem there."

"Well then, the thing to do is have fun and drop him the day school starts."

"Willie, that's a terrible thing to say. I'd never do that."

"You did it to Kip."

"I did not."

"Have you told him yet?"

"He's coming home tomorrow for a couple of days. I'll tell him then."

"Don't," Willie said. "Just let it slide. Summer will be over soon and we'll all be back to normal."

"I'm going to tell him," Ellynne said. "And I have to tell you that I don't think we'll all be back to normal when summer is over. I think I'm really stuck on him."

"Kip?"

"Kenny. You know I mean Kenny."

"I was just hoping, Sweetie," Willie said and then she sighed. "Think about it carefully, Ellynne. Kip is an awful nice guy."

Ellynne dreaded seeing Kip at all. When he knocked on the door of their apartment, she quickly kissed him on the cheek, happy that her mother was in the room so she could avoid a more enthusiastic embrace. Indeed, Judith greeted him much more warmly than she ever had, spending a long time asking him questions about his work.

"I've wondered about the inner workings of Disneyland ever since I went there," Judith said. "Now I know a real insider who can give me the straight scoop. Is it true they have robots inside some of the animals that walk around and talk to the kids?"

"Not as far as I know," Kip answered. "The people who are hired to do that job look perfectly real to me. Except when they come out of the suits they look awful sweaty. They say it's one of the toughest jobs because it's so hot inside the furry suits. The plastic ones are worse."

"The jungle boat ride must be a lot of fun," Judith said. "I loved it the day I was there."

"It's still one of the most popular rides," Kip said, "even though it's one of the oldest. I guess it's one that people like to work on too. Doesn't scare the little kids or anything, so it's pretty easy except when the lines get too long. On July 4th the line was over two hours long, at least part of the time."

Judith shuddered. "I wouldn't stand in line two hours if they were giving away solid gold lions and tigers."

"People come from a long way off and they only have a day or two. We get them from everywhere, even China."

Kip and her mother really seemed to enjoy talking with each other and Ellynne was grateful that she didn't have to do more than listen as they chatted about work and law school. Most of the time she just sat quietly on the couch, listening to them and looking at Kip. He was the same wonderful, handsome boy she'd fallen for last fall, but the feeling she had tonight was totally different.

I'm a different person, Ellynne told herself, and she knew that Kenny had something to do with that difference. With Kenny, she'd learned to enjoy her life in a new way, she'd learned there was more to life than just working hard and saving money. She felt helpless to ever try and explain it to her mother or Kip or any of her friends, but she was sure that Kenny was a very important teacher for her. Yet, she knew if anyone asked her what she'd learned this summer, she would have to say, "Nothing."

As for her feelings about Kip, they were changed too. She was nervous about seeing him and dreaded telling him about Kenny, but except for that, she didn't seem to be feeling much of anything. Kip was still darling, with dark brown hair that curled around his ears and deep, clear blue eyes. His smile was the same warm, contagious smile it had always been, and though he seemed a little tired and a little more grown up, he really hadn't changed a bit. *It's me*, Ellynne decided. *I'm the one who's changed.*

Finally, Kip stood up and asked, "Want to take a drive, Ellynne?"

"Sure," she said calmly, but her heart was in her throat as she followed him out of the house. *Sooner or later, I'll have to tell him about Kenny. It might as well be sooner*, she decided.

"Where to?" Kip asked.

"Let's just drive around and talk for a while," Ellynne said.

Kip drove up to Palos Verdes and parked at the look-out point where they could see the Los Angeles harbor and the lights surrounding it. He took her in his arms and kissed her. Ellynne felt nervous and embarrassed and she wasn't able to hide her feelings from Kip.

"What's wrong, Ellynne?" he asked. "Are you mad at me?

"No, of course not, Kip."

"Something is bothering you, though, right?"

"Well, yeah. I mean, sort of. . . ." Her voice trailed off. She couldn't look Kip in the eyes.

"Do you want to talk about it?" he asked gently.

"No . . . but. . . ." She could feel her eyes start to sting with tears. ". . . I have to." She looked up then and saw Kip looking down at her with a worried look on his face.

"I met someone, Kip," Ellynne said very quietly. "I never expected it to happen, but we started dating and . . . and, well, I really like him a lot."

"I see," he said after a moment.

There was another long silence and Ellynne found that she was waiting impatiently for Kip to respond. It occurred to her that he sometimes was as heavy and serious as an old man. Funny how just a few months ago she would have given anything just to have him smile at her and now . . . now she wasn't sure how she felt except that when she was with Kenny, she had more fun.

Finally, Kip cleared his throat and said in a strained voice, "I was afraid of this when you didn't have anything to do all summer and I went to Disneyland. I knew it was a risk and it looks like I lost, at least for the time being. Is this serious? This thing between you and . . ."

"Kenny," she supplied. "It's pretty serious, Kip. I'm going with him."

"Where did you meet him?" Kip asked.

"At the beach."

"Is he a lifeguard?"

"No. He's just at the beach. We got friendly and then it . . . it progressed."

Kip nodded solemnly. "Things progress, I guess."

But if Kip noticed that he'd made a rhyme, he ignored it and went on. "Look Ellynne, there's really nothing much I can do from here. I've got another five weeks to work and I need the job. I might get another couple of days off but basically, I'm stuck till Labor

Day. But when school starts, things may look different. Maybe it's just a summer romance."

Her primary reaction was shock. Summer vacation would only last five more weeks. How had the time gone so fast? But just because school would start was no reason to believe she wouldn't be seeing Kenny. They could see each other almost every weekend. She knew his crowd gathered on the beach on warm days during Christmas vacation and really started in earnest during Easter week.

"Maybe we can start dating again in September. Maybe I can challenge Kenny to a duel. I'll get you back, without a doubt." Kip's effort at a lightheartedness was spoiled by the catch in his voice.

"I don't think so." Ellynne fought to keep from crying and to be honest with Kip. *Think about Kenny*, she told herself and his face appeared in her mind. There he was, smiling that mocking smile, and his light blue eyes burned into her, giving her strength. She thought about how close she felt to Kenny when they sat and talked like this. With Kip, right now, she felt a tremendous gap, as though they were miles apart. Yet Kip had been her beloved boyfriend only a few weeks ago. What had happened?

"Maybe you were subconsciously angry because I went to work," Kip said.

"No."

"Or you just wanted to experiment a little bit. We agreed that we weren't going steady this summer so maybe nothing at all has happened."

"Something's happened," Ellynne said dully. She shivered and wrapped her arms around herself, saying, "I feel terrible."

"You should feel how *I* feel," Kip said, trying to make a joke. Then he pulled her close to him and kissed her fiercely. Pulling back, he said, "I'll be around, Ellynne. I'll be around."

Ellynne was silent because she didn't know what else to say. Her head told her that Kip might be right, that she might get over Kenny when school started and she picked up her ordinary life, but she didn't really believe it. "We'll see," Ellynne said, and she told herself that she had been fair to Kip by telling him about Kenny. Then she thought about how beautiful Kenny was and how happy she felt when she was with him. When she was with Kip, things were too serious. "I'm really crazy about this guy," she added, knowing for the first time how completely true that was.

When Kip let her out of the car, he asked, "I'd like to see you again. I've got two days off."

"I just told you I was going with Kenny."

"Well you must have started dating Kenny when you were going with me," Kip said, sarcastically. "Turn about's fair play." He looked at her appraisingly and said, "If you change your mind, call me. Vacation will be over in five weeks and I'll be around a long time after that."

She slipped into the house quietly but her mother was still awake, watching television. Judith called out to her, "Kip with you?"

Ellynne opened the door to her mother's room and said, "I have something to tell you."

Her mother flipped off the TV by remote control and patted the edge of the bed. "What happened?"

"I told Kip I was dating someone else," Ellynne began.

Judith frowned and asked, "Why did you do that?"

"Because I am. Or at least I'm seeing a lot of him mostly on the beach. His name is Kenny and he's going to be a college student this fall. I've had him over a couple of times when you were at school," she confessed.

Judith asked, "Is there more to this that I should know?"

It took her a minute to understand what her mother was asking her and then she answered, "No. That's all there is to it. He's a real nice guy, Mother, and I'm having a lot of fun with him. I just wasn't sure how serious I was about him, so I didn't see any real reason to mention him until now."

Instead of the lecture and argument she expected, her mother nodded and said, "I'm glad you decided to tell me now. As for your having him here when I'm not here, I'm not going to start making rules for you now, Ellynne. You're a big girl and a smart one. I would like to meet your friend, though."

Relieved that her mother had been so reasonable, Ellynne promised, "Soon. Maybe tomorrow."

As she stood up to go to her own room, her mother asked, "You say you're *going with* this Kenny. Where are you going?"

"What do you mean?"

"You're home every night. Doesn't he ever take you anywhere?"

"I see a lot of him at the beach," Ellynne explained though she wasn't convinced that her mother accepted the explanation because as Ellynne shut the door, she heard her mother mumbling to herself.

The words were, "Going no place isn't going together." And then, very distinctly, Ellynne heard her mother say, "Poor Kip."

N_ine_

"Dinner?" Kenny asked. "Do I have to wear a suit and one of those things . . . ?" He placed two hands around his neck and pretended to be choking himself.

"Just a tee-shirt and jeans," Ellynne assured him. "My mom's not very fancy."

"But formal," Kenny objected. "I can tell by the furniture. All that old stuff." He pretended to shudder and said, "Reminds me of the old movies on TV. You know, the ones where the house turns out to not be haunted after all."

"A lot of the furniture is from our family. There's more in storage."

Kenny pretended to shudder again and then asked seriously, "Why did your mom keep all that old stuff?"

"It's valuable and it reminded her of the past, I guess. She likes it." Ellynne did not add that she had personally selected the pieces she loved most for her own bedroom and that her dreams of the future included a house that was filled with wonderful antiques. She knew that Kenny's aversion to old things was typical of many Californians' attitudes toward decoration. Even Willie's family, who could afford anything they wanted, had chosen the most modern decor they could find rather than antiques. Yet Ellynne loved the old woods, the soft colors and the well-worn look of her family furniture, and she was a little annoyed that Kenny didn't appreciate it.

"I'm not usually so accomodating," Kenny assured her as he kissed the tip of her nose, "but for my girl, I'll make the effort."

"Good. Seven tonight. And will you do me another favor?"

"What, my fair damsel?"

"Try not to joke around too much. My mom's kind of . . . serious."

Kenny raised one eyebrow and said, "I could have told you that by the furniture. The first time I set foot inside that place I said to myself, now this is the house of a *serious* person. It's a good thing you met me, Ellynne, or your life might have been ruined by *seriosity*."

She laughed but she also shook her head and insisted, "Promise."

"I promise."

Ellynne relaxed, then lay back on her beach towel and looked up at the sky. There were some small white clouds chasing their tails around in the blue sky and she amused herself imagining they were sheep, then fish, and later birds. As she looked at the sky, she could hear the sound of the waves working as a steady rhythm against all the other sounds on the beach; the portable radios, the shouts of children, and the calling of sea gulls all blended into a beach music that was enchanting to Ellynne.

She stretched her arms overhead and sat up, saying, "I feel exactly like one of those clouds."

"You look better," Kenny assured her. "Want to go for a bike ride?"

"Sure."

They rode all the way to Hermosa Beach and back and then Ellynne went home to prepare for the supper she'd planned. As she cooked, she listened to the radio and even sang along with it while she chopped onions. After serious consideration, she'd decided on a chicken marengo recipe that she'd tried twice before. That, with a salad and ice cream for dessert, would be simple and easy. Ellynne wanted to avoid any difficulties, and choosing a simple menu had seemed like the first step in that plan.

As she finished up the chicken marengo and put it in the oven for an hour's slow baking, she realized that the oven was heating the apartment, making it seem smaller and hotter than usual. She wiped the sweat from her forehead and decided to take a shower, though she'd already had two today, one in the morning and one after she came in from her bike ride.

Showering made her feel better and she was almost relaxed when Judith came in from school. Her mother's first words were, "Smells good."

"Apartment too hot?" she asked. Before she'd taken her shower, she'd opened the silding glass doors to the small patio and the ocean breeze, which was always cool, seemed to have cleared out most of the heat.

"Just right." Her mother went into her bedroom and Ellynne could hear the shower running. When she came out, she was wearing a pair of short shorts and a tee-shirt. She had no shoes on.

Ellynne giggled as she said, "I asked him to wear long pants and a tee-shirt."

"Even shoes?" her mother teased and disappeared again. This time when she returned, she looked more like her normal self in a pair of cotton pants and a blouse. Her hair, which was usually pulled back in a bun, was tied loosely with a white ribbon and she was wearing thongs.

"You look great," Ellynne said. Now if her mother would just act as young and carefree as she looked, everything would be fine.

Kenny rang the bell promptly at seven and Ellynne noted with relief that he was wearing a nice pair of light blue denim Levis and a light blue tee-shirt with a small yellow stripe. It looked brand-new and she wondered if he'd gone out and bought clothes for the occasion. Then she decided they were probably ones he'd never bothered to put on. Kenny's idea of being well dressed was having thongs in the same color. One thing she loved about him was that he seemed totally and absolutely unconcerned about his appearance.

Ellynne thought the first half of the evening went rather well, partly because Kenny and her mother both seemed to spend a lot of time talking about her delicious dinner and what a good cook she was. Ellynne was pleased but cynical enough to know that part of the praise was simply a way of filling in the conversation with a safe topic.

After supper, Kenny offered to help with the dishes but Ellynne shook her head and sent him into the livingroom to talk with her mother. She rinsed things off quickly and put them in the dishwasher, hoping that nothing would go awry while they were alone. She wasn't sure exactly what she feared, but she supposed that they were such different types that they would inevitably clash.

When she got into the livingroom Judith was telling Kenny about her classes at law school and he was leaning back, looking quite comfortable in the blue velvet wing chair, sipping his coffee and acting as if he had conversations like this one every day.

Ellynne breathed a sigh of relief and sat down on the couch next to her mother. Things were going well.

But Judith seemed to think it was time to switch to subjects of more general interest, so she said, "That's enough legal talk. What are you studying in school?"

"I'm not exactly sure," Kenny answered, shifting the coffee cup from saucer to his mouth, then setting them both down on the table without drinking. "I've thought about a career in law myself."

Ellynne gulped. In all the time she'd known Kenny, she'd never heard him talk about future plans at all.

Judith nodded. "They say there's going to be a glut of lawyers in the next ten years, but I think there's always room for someone who's sharp and willing to compete. I knew things would be tight when I started out but it was what I wanted to do. I think the most compelling reason to choose a career is a deep desire, don't you?"

"Yes," Kenny answered. "Actually, that's the reason I've held off making a decision. I don't have a burning desire at this time but I expect I will have sometime soon."

Judith nodded her head. "That's what I tell Ellynne. Just experiment until you find the right thing. Too many kids fall into the trap of doing what their parents do or going the way their counselors think is best. I want Ellynne to really explore during her liberal arts years. Time enough to specialize in graduate school."

Ellynne flushed. She had never told Kenny she had such ambitious plans for college.

None of the other kids ever seemed very interested in school so she just hadn't talked about it. But she could see by the cool amusement in Kenny's eyes that he was finding his conversation with her mother very illuminating. He asked, "Is Ellynne planning to go to graduate school?"

"I hope so," Judith answered. "But the first thing is to get accepted to an Ivy League undergraduate program."

"Ivy League?"

Ellynne wondered if Kenny even knew what the phrase meant, but her mother assumed he was asking which one, so she answered, "She's applied to Princeton, Brown, and Yale."

Now Ellynne was distinctly aware of the amusement in Kenny's eyes, but her mother saw nothing and continued to brag about her plans for her daughter. "Her father went to Yale and I know it would have made him very proud to have his daughter accepted to his alma mater. Of course, we never talked about it because young women weren't accepted to those schools in our day."

"Really? I didn't know that."

Judith looked surprised and she slowed down as she said, "Well, I suppose you westerners don't really pay as much attention to such things as we did in the east, but the Ivy League schools were all just for men until the 1970's. I can remember when the first women started as freshmen, how excited we all were."

"Why were you excited?" Kenny asked. Ellynne's heart sank because the question betrayed his lack of interest in political and social issues in a way that her mother would not be able to miss.

Judith Aleese's voice was very reserved now as she said, "We were excited because it meant a giant step forward for women. The admission of females to the private bastions of power was the beginning of the end for the eastern male establishment. It meant eventual admission to the Old Boy network. . . ." She broke off and tried to laugh as she changed the subject, "But I wanted to hear about *your* plans, not bore you with my views. What sort of courses are you taking now?"

"It's summer," Kenny said. "I don't start school till September."

"But you must have your curriculum selected?"

Kenny shrugged and then seemed to make an effort to remember, "English, history, math, stuff like that."

"I should think your affinity for the sea would make you interested in oceanography," Judith offered.

"Did I tell you that Kenny and I saw some dolphins the other day?" Ellynne asked.

"No."

Judith turned to Kenny, obviously expecting him to elaborate on the adventure but he only said, "There must have been a dozen of them."

"They were beautiful," Ellynne said. "They played for a long time, almost like they were skipping rope or something, the way they jumped up and down in a circle."

"They're really playful fish," Kenny added. "I saw some others on my surfboard once. They hung around a long time. Really close too."

Ellynne wished he hadn't called them fish in front of her mother. She knew her mother was judging him all the time and that he'd definitely come out lacking in the education department, during the conversation about colleges. She sighed and told herself that things had worked out better than she'd had any right to expect. Conversation had been polite, dinner had been good, and neither her mother nor Kenny had actually disgraced themselves.

Kenny left at nine-fifteen after assuring them both that he'd had a wonderful time. Ellynne walked him down to the street where he kissed her and whispered, "Some kids are getting together to party about ten tonight. Come on down."

"I don't think so," Ellynne answered. "My mom would have a fit if she knew I was partying on the beach. You should hear what our neighbors say about your friends' beach parties."

Kenny shook his head and said, "That's what I get for running around with a member of the ruling class."

"What's that supposed to mean?"

"I didn't know you were on your way to Yale," Kenny said. "I thought you were a cute cheerleader turned beach bum."

"Almost cheerleader," she reminded him and then she laughed and hugged him, saying, "I'm that too. But there are a lot of parts to me, Kenny, and I want you to know all of them."

He squeezed her arms, then her waist and said, "I like some of those parts and others just drive me wild." He buried his face in her neck and pretended to bite as he said in a Dracula voice, "Pretty maiden, come to the party. I turn into a beast about midnight, especially in the full moon. You should be there to enjoy the show."

She stepped back laughing as he blew hard on her neck, making a funny sound and sending shivers up and down her spine. She was still laughing as she said, "I can't and besides, from what I hear about your famous parties, you really do turn into a beast. I worry about you."

"Nothing to worry about," he assured her. "By daylight, I'll be your regular all-American beach bum again. Your mom really faked me out with all that talk about future plans."

"I think things went well. Thanks for being so sensible."

"Sensible? You want sensible? You ain't seen sensible yet. Wait till the next time. Next time I'll walk right in and sit right down and say, 'Cut the conversation, where's the beef?' That's sensible."

Ellynne was still laughing as she walked into her apartment and her mother asked, "What's funny?"

"Kenny. He makes me laugh."

Judith nodded her head and added, "And I must say I had no idea he would be so handsome. He's absolutely, breathtakingly beautiful. I guess every girl is entitled to one brainless beauty in her life."

"What do you mean?"

"I just mean if we're really going to be liberated then I guess we're entitled to make the same stupid mistakes that men do."

"Are you saying that Kenny's stupid or I am?"

"Calm down, Ellynne," Judith's voice sounded tired and cautious. "I just meant he was absolutely, breathtakingly handsome, that's all."

"But you implied he was stupid."

"I implied nothing. You're reacting to what he said this evening. I must say I was more impressed than I expected."

"You expected him to make a fool of himself, that's why you gave him the third degree."

"I definitely did *not* give him the third degree. I did everything in my power to draw him into the conversation, and if you're uncomfortable with what he said, that's your problem, not mine."

"There are more important things in this world than what college a person goes to," Ellynne said. "I was embarrassed by all that talk about Yale."

Judith's eyes were flaring now and she snapped her answer, "If you wanted to know why I'm really worried about your running about with that . . . that beach boy . . . it's because of exactly that. I don't want his values to dissuade you from getting into the best school possible. Don't fall into the trap, Ellynne. Don't fall for some guy and let him ruin your life."

"You come up with some of the weirdest worries about me." Ellynne was practically shouting. "Now you think I'm going to get married and drop out of high school just because I took the summer off. You don't think that's a little exaggerated?"

"I suppose so," Judith conceded. "But Ellynne, wouldn't you be worried if your daughter were going out with someone who has such a different lifestyle?"

"Not if I trusted my daughter," Ellynne answered. She went to her room and came back in a minute with her red windbreaker.

"Where are you going?" her mother asked.

"I'm meeting Kenny and some others at the beach. They're having a party."

She expected her mother to say she couldn't go and she was determined that she would, but Judith simply asked, "Why didn't he ask you to go when he was here?"

"He asked me earlier and I forgot to tell you."

Judith looked as though she had more to say but her only words were, "Have a good time."

"I'll be in around midnight or a little later," Ellynne offered.

"I'll be asleep," her mother answered. "See you in the morning."

Ellynne walked out of the house, hoping that the anger she felt would be strong enough to propel her all the way down to Avenue C. Like most of the quarrels she had with her mother, the heat flared fast and then was dispelled quickly, but she needed some of that heat now to give her the courage to go to the beach party, a party she knew would be illegal, not only because it was after hours at the beach, but because a lot of the kids who would be drinking were under age.

Ten

She walked quickly, ignoring the few people who were still walking or riding their bikes on the boardwalk. Though there were enough people around for it still to be quite safe, Ellynne knew that she would have to get a ride home later in the evening. The darkness brought danger to a pretty young girl.

There were a few dark shapes sitting in exactly the same spot that the group occupied in the daytime so Ellynne turned off the boardwalk at the Avenue C steps and started towards them, assuming they would be friends. At night, everything felt and looked different. Even walking over the sand seemed more difficult and Ellynne had the feeling that the distance between the dark shapes outlined against the horizon and the board-walk had tripled in the night.

When she got closer she recognized Davy, Gloria and a young man she didn't know.

There were only three others and she didn't know them either. "Where's Kenny?" she asked.

"Gone with Sailor for beer," Gloria answered. "Meet Bill."

Ellynne continued standing, suddenly feeling that she had made a terrible mistake even coming to this party. The cold night air was damp and she wished she'd worn a heavier jacket. Her red windbreaker was all right as long as she was moving but the idea of sitting down on the damp sand with nothing more than the windbreaker for warmth didn't appeal to her.

She could make out in the dim light that one of the boys was shirtless and that Gloria had on shorts and a sleeveless tee-shirt. She and her mother were convinced that many Californians went around chronically cold because they didn't wear enough clothing. When they'd first moved here, Judith had said, "All my life I've heard people talk about people who were *overdressed* but this is the first place I've ever been where it's in style to *underdress*."

"Sit down," Gloria said.

"I should have brought a blanket," Ellynne said. Then she added, "Kenny invited me."

"He'll be here in a minute," Gloria assured her. "He went to the liquor store with Sailor."

She didn't seem to notice that she'd just repeated herself and no one made any attempt to say anything else. Over to the side, sitting on a different blanket, one of the other fellows that she didn't know said, "You alone? Come on over here."

"I'm waiting for my boyfriend," Ellynne said.

"Come on over anyway," the boy laughed and motioned with his hand. "Kenny won't care. Kenny's a good guy."

Ellynne shook her head but realized she could not continue to stand while the others sat so she sank to the sand, crossing her legs in a lotus position. Gloria sighed and said, "You would have made a great cheerleader."

She wondered if Kenny had been talking about her and then remembered that Gloria had been a part-time student at Redondo High last year. Gloria's voice was soft as she repeated herself, "Great cheerleader." After a long silence, she added, "I wanted to be a cheerleader when I was a little girl too."

"Did you try out?" Ellynne asked.

"Wouldn't have done any good," Gloria said. "They always pick popular girls like you."

"They didn't pick me," Ellynne reminded her. She was annoyed that Gloria seemed to think all you had to do was be popular to make the team. She added, "I worked really hard before the tryouts too."

"I wanted to be a cheerleader," Gloria repeated. "But I'm not like you. You're lucky."

"I worked hard and I didn't make it," Ellynne answered. Then she decided that

Gloria would probably never understand that people who looked lucky were often people who'd put a lot of time and effort in. She thought about Willie, for instance. Willie always looked as though things came easily for her, but Willie struggled with some school subjects and being black certainly made things harder for her. But Ellynne was willing to bet that Gloria thought she had it a lot harder than Willie did.

"What do you want to be now that you're a big girl?" Davy asked.

"Just me," Gloria said and sighed deeply, "Just Gloria." She lay back and looked up at the sky. "Look at all those stars."

The two boys lay back beside her and obediently looked up at the sky. One of them, although Ellynne wasn't sure whether it was Davy or Bill, said, "Lots of stars."

The others said "Yeah," and there was another long silence.

Ellynne told herself she shouldn't have even bothered trying to make conversation with them because they didn't really have anything interesting to say. The two boys who were sitting on the other blanket called out to her again, "Come on over."

The damp sand was very cold now and she decided she might as well join them on their blanket. Kenny would be here soon to rescue her so there was no harm, especially since they knew him. She got up, walked over, and sat down again. One of the boys who had shoulder-length hair looked familiar, but she didn't know his name. She didn't think she'd ever seen the other one before.

The one with shoulder-length hair said, "Elaine, this is my buddy from Malibu. Great surfer."

She said, "Hi, I'm Ellynne," but she wasn't sure if either one of them heard the way she pronounced her name and neither of them introduced themselves.

"You're a good-looking girl, Elaine," the one from Malibu said. "What you want to hang around with a rat like Sailor for?"

"I'm Ellynne and I'm with Kenny."

"Come closer," the shoulder-length-haired one said. "You don't need to be cold."

He reached for her arm and Ellynne pulled away quickly, jumping up and saying, "Guess I'll go now."

"Come on over here," the two fellows called in unison as she walked toward the boardwalk. "We won't bother you," the one with shoulder-length hair promised.

"Kenny's a friend of mine," the other called. "Don't run away."

Ellynne ignored their calls but when one of them called out, "Scaredy cat, scaredy cat," she found that she was really angry. She hated the idea that she was letting two idiots run her away from a party. Ordinarily she would have stood her ground but she had no idea what kind of people they were. If she confronted them, she might get into more than she bargained for.

She wasn't sure whether she was happy or sad when she saw Sailor and ChooChoo at the top of the Avenue C stairs. She might have kept on going except she was sure that Kenny had to be with them. She was afraid he would worry about her if he knew she had been there and left. She stood at the bottom of the stairs and listened to ChooChoo and Sailor arguing as they carried large paper bags down.

"All I asked for were some potato chips," ChooChoo was complaining. "You'd think I asked for a diamond ring or something."

"I'll get you a diamond ring," Sailor answered. His voice sounded different, as though he were an old married man who had been listening to his wife complain for thirty years. Ellynne almost wanted to laugh, this Sailor was so unlike the bragging Sailor she knew.

"You said that last winter," ChooChoo answered. "It's not just the potato chips or the ring," she took a deep breath and began again, "It's your whole attitude, Sailor. I'm tired of sitting around waiting for you to grow up."

"You know what?" Sailor said, "I'm sick of your nagging. I wish I'd bought the chips so you'd have your mouth too full to talk. Come on, honey, this is a party."

"Party. That's all you care about. You don't care about me at all."

Ellynne was embarrassed for them, especially for the usually silent ChooChoo. She hated to have them know she'd heard their argument but she knew they'd discover her very soon anyway. She called up, "Hi, it's me, Ellynne. Ellynne Aleese."

She walked back to the party with them after learning that Kenny was following in ChooChoo's car. "He said he'd stop for gas at this station where he knows the guy," ChooChoo explained, as she opened a paper bag and pulled out a can of Coke. Popping the top off of it, she offered it to Ellynne.

Ellynne nodded her head. "Sure."

"I don't drink either," ChooChoo explained. "Can't really afford to when Sailor's around."

Ellynne wasn't sure whether she meant she couldn't afford to drink because she had to take care of her boyfriend when he drank too much or because she had to buy his beer. She knew that ChooChoo worked in a record shop sometimes and that she always had money. ChooChoo seemed to resent spending her earnings on Sailor but she never really said no. Now Ellynne wondered if it was just that ChooChoo didn't talk much in front of other people. That conversation she'd just overheard sounded a lot like some of the arguments she had with her mother — every line was so well worn it was like a familiar movie.

They sat on blankets, talking very little while the damp air curled around them and began to bore into their bones. Ellynne was uncomfortable, not only because of the weather, but because the party wasn't much fun. Gloria and her two friends were so silly, they contributed only giggles. ChooChoo never talked and Sailor was so busy bragging to the guy from Malibu that Ellynne was pretty sure she could get up and leave without anyone noticing it.

She wanted to at least wait for Kenny, but the cold air was getting to her and she was bored by Sailor's talk. Once, she turned to ChooChoo and asked, "Do you like working in the record store?"

"Sort of," ChooChoo answered, but she didn't elaborate.

"I think the customers would be nice," Ellynne said. "I mean, they probably all like music and are happy to be in there buying things."

"Sometimes," ChooChoo agreed.

"I have a friend who's working at Disneyland this summer and he says the people are fun to wait on because they're all on vacation. He says when your customers are having fun, you have fun too. Not like pulling teeth."

"What?"

"You know, like dentists pull teeth and people hate them."

"People don't hate dentists."

"It was kind of a joke," Ellynne started to explain that she hadn't really meant that people hated dentists but she was hoping all the time that Kenny would come down the stairs and rescue her. Funny how easy it was for her to talk to Kenny and how hard it was for

119

her to talk to his friends. But she'd figured out a long time ago that Kenny was really a lot smarter than most of his friends. Nicer too.

She let her conversation with ChooChoo collapse and tuned in to Sailor's eternal bragging about surfing. ". . . so I come into the center of the section and the other guy comes from his side — there was no way I was going to let that outlander have that wave and we're coming nearer and nearer to the section. . . ."

Ellynne had learned enough to know that the section was the place where two waves met, forming a kind of v in the water. She also knew that surfers had an unwritten rule that the guy who caught the wave first had it, but Sailor was bragging about how tough he was on a board.

". . . so we meet in the section and my board is tallest. I'd tried my best to keep it up and my board comes down on that guy's head and we're in washing machine. I mean it was a tall one — about ten feet — and I never saw that guy again."

Ellynne shuddered even though she knew it was probably a big lie.

After a while, Ellynne decided that Kenny must not be coming and she said as much to the others. Sailor waved a hand and said, "Naw, he'll be here. He just had to stop by his house and check on his mother."

"Is she sick?" Ellynne asked.

"You didn't tell me he was going all the way to North Redondo in my car," ChooChoo said. She used the same nagging tone that Ellynne had heard earlier.

Sailor made a noise deep in his throat and continued his surfing stories. Ellynne shivered and hugged herself. What had started out as defiance against her mother had turned into a really bad time. Somehow, when she'd imagined their beach parties, she'd imagined music and food and fun but this was a disaster. Why did they talk the next day about what a great time they'd had?

She walked up to the streetlight once and looked at her watch. It was almost midnight, which meant she'd been waiting for Kenny over an hour. To be honest, Ellynne had to admit that he had no way of knowing she was there, but she was going to have to leave soon, because she was freezing and it was very late. She hated to walk home alone this late at night but she wondered if that wouldn't be the best idea. She was feeling angry with herself for coming to this stupid party and ashamed because she knew she'd done it against her better judgment, just because she was mad at her mother.

As she was trying to decide whether to walk home alone, Kenny called out from the bottom of the stairs, "I'm home at last." He was carrying beer and seemed really pleased with himself when he dropped it on the blanket. Then he grabbed Ellynne around the waist and kissed her as he tossed the car keys to ChooChoo.

"I waited almost two hours," she said. Did her voice sound as angry and whiney as ChooChoo's? She hoped not.

"Sorry honey," Kenny squeezed her round the waist.

"I have to go home," Ellynne said.

"You just got here," Kenny said, patting her on the head as though she were an impatient child.

"No, *you* just got here."

Ellynne realized that she had a new problem — one that had not occurred to her earlier. She really didn't want to ride with Kenny anymore because he had obviously been drinking. For the hundredth time that evening, Ellynne wished she'd never come to the party.

She stood up and asked, "Kenny, will you walk me home?"

"Later, Ellynne. Sit down."

"I'm going to walk home alone, then."

"Just sit down and be a good girl, like ChooChoo," Kenny said.

His words made her furious — at least as furious as she'd been earlier in the evening with her mother. She turned on her heel and started across the dark sand. It occurred to her that the circumstances under which she was leaving the party were just about exactly the same as the way she'd arrived.

"Wait up, Ellynne." It was ChooChoo's voice in the dark.

Ellynne slowed down but she was determined she was going home now, no matter what. But instead of arguing with her, ChooChoo offered her a ride.

They climbed the stairs and walked to ChooChoo's car in silence but once inside, when ChooChoo started the motor, she said, "This is the last time I come to one of these things."

"It's not a whole lot of fun." Ellynne agreed. She was feeling almost lightheaded with relief now that she was finally leaving and riding home with a sober driver.

They pulled away from the parking place and started down the street. "I want some potato chips," ChooChoo said as an explanation for turning off the Esplanade and onto a side street.

As they turned the corner, Ellynne saw a police car coming from the other direction. The car passed them and turned right. "Good thing we left," ChooChoo said.

"Have you ever been at a party when the police came?" Ellynne asked.

"Practically every time. That's usually the way they get broken up."

"What happens?"

"Usually they just flash their lights and everybody scatters. Then they go home. You know they're all spoiled brats."

$E^{\underline{leven}}$

"Spoiled brat," Ellynne accused Kenny as they sat on the edge of the iron railing of her apartment patio. It was five o'clock in the afternoon and Kenny had come to talk with her after she hadn't shown up on the beach that day.

"Don't make a big deal out of it," he answered. "So the party was a bust, so what?"

"It was almost a different kind of bust," Ellynne was still angry, partly at herself for going to the beach party in the first place and partly at Kenny's stubborn insistence that she was the one with a problem.

"A different kind of bust?" Kenny raised his eyebrows and wiggled them, trying to look as much like Groucho Marx as possible. "Where is she? Lead me to her."

"It just isn't funny," Ellynne said. "It was kind of sad, really. All you guys sitting around in a circle, telling lies and drinking too much. Like a bunch of bums. Kenny, you're too good for that."

"You're right," Kenny said. Trying to grab her and bring her into his arms, he said in a dramatic voice, "You're right. I'm too good for this life. Take me away, Ellynne — take me away from it all. Let's flee to Tahiti together."

Despite herself, Ellynne laughed as she pushed him away. "I just want you to be still one minute and listen to what I'm saying. Then I have to cook supper."

"Supper?"

"You can stay if you want. Mom will be here around seven."

"Are you having ice cream and cookies?" When she shook her head, he asked, "Sauerbraten and cabbage?"

"Fish and broccoli. If you stay I'll fry some potatoes."

"Can't," Kenny said. "I've got other fish to fry."

"Stay," Ellynne said. "Then after supper we can go to the movies." She added, "I'll treat."

"I can't." He kissed her cheek and then her forehead. Nuzzling her neck he whispered, "I'm glad you're not mad at me anymore. I hate it when you're mad at me."

"I am mad at you," Ellynne said. "I think last night was stupid and I'm tired of just seeing you on the beach. I think we should go places, do things. Do you know my summer's almost over and I haven't done anything?"

"Except fall in love with me," Kenny teased. "I'd say that was a monumental happening."

"You said we'd go to San Clemente."

"When I get my car fixed."

"Then why don't you get your car fixed?"

"No bread."

She was furious again, she realized. Her eyes blazed as she said, "Then why don't you get a job and earn enough money to get your car fixed?"

"You sound a lot like my mother," Kenny said. "Are you sure you're only fifteen years old?"

"Are you sure you're not three?"

He shook his head and said, "Ellynne, life's a lot too short to argue with my best girl. I'll see you tomorrow at the beach. O.K.?"

"Maybe," Ellynne capitulated.

Kenny held her close. This time he was absolutely serious as he said, "I really hate it when you're mad at me, Ellynne." He kissed her. "I need you," Kenny said. "And I don't want to lose you but I don't want you to try and change me either."

She couldn't resist asking again, "Are you sure you don't want to stay for supper? We could go for a walk later."

"Your mom makes me nervous," Kenny admitted. "Plus, I hate fish. See you."

She watched him from the balcony as he came down the stairs, climbed on his bicycle and pedaled down the boardwalk. His golden hair was like a fiery cap of orange in the red light of the late day sun and his broad shoulders and back gleamed as though they were fashioned in bronze. He looked a lot like one of those Greek statues of the perfect man, Ellynne decided.

While she was dipping the fish in cornmeal, the telephone rang and she answered with one hand while she continued to turn the fish with the other. It was Kip, who said, "I was just in town for the day and wondered if I could come over for a while. I've got a new John Lee Hooker album."

On their first date, Ellynne and Kip had discovered that they were both blues enthusiasts and she was pretty certain that his offering to spend the evening listening was an attempt to bring back memories of their first times together. She hesitated, wondering if it would be fair to Kip to say yes.

"Just thought I'd give it a try," Kip's voice was determined.

"I'm still dating Kenny," she answered.

"I didn't ask you that. Look, we could go to the movies, or bowling or something if you're scared I'll breathe too heavy."

"Yes." Ellynne dropped the fish into the popping grease in her black frying pan. She was touched by Kip's attempt to joke and she was tired of sitting home every night.

"Where?"

"Anywhere," Ellynne answered. "Anywhere at all."

Kip picked her up at eight-thirty and they went to a nine o'clock movie at the mall. When they drove back to her apartment, he said, "Not a very exciting evening. I'll try to do better next time."

"It was fun for me," Ellynne said. "My mother spends all her time studying and with Willie working such early hours, I haven't been anywhere all summer."

Kip looked at her curiously. "What about Kenny?" Then he grinned and shook his head, "I swore I wasn't going to mention his name once tonight."

"Kenny and I mostly hang out on the beach," Ellynne admitted. Then, before Kip got his hopes up, she added, "I'm having a wonderful summer doing nothing but I've really learned to love the water. You should see me ride the waves."

"Have you tried surfing?" Kip asked.

"Once," Ellynne admitted, "but I fell right off. I guess I should try some more, but it seemed like too much work to learn. I've enjoyed being lazy, so I've just hung out."

"What do you think about?" Kip asked. "I stopped going to the beach because I would lie on the sand and be bored to death. It didn't really relax me."

"I don't really think," Ellynne said. "I mostly just look at the water and watch it move. It turns colors and it's sort of like dancing. It's hard to explain."

"You're a nature lover. That's not hard to understand."

"I love it all," Ellynne said. "The sand and the sun and even the seaweed. But I don't want to *do* anything with it. I mean, Willie thinks she wants to be an oceanographer and she hates the beach. I'd bet anything that I'll end up in an office or classroom but I'll always visit the beach on weekends. I think it's the most beautiful thing in the world."

Kip put his arms around her and drew her closer to him, saying, "Maybe you fell in love with the Pacific Ocean, not Kenny. Maybe I could learn to love the beach again if I was with you. Want me to teach you to surf?"

Ellynne laughed and shook her head, "I don't think it's that simple." Then she asked, "Do you surf?"

"Of course," Kip answered. "Just about every California kid learns to surf a little bit."

"Didn't you like it?"

"I loved it when I was in junior high, but after the tenth grade I just lost interest. I started playing football and I was always working on weekends so I stopped surfing. I guess I got too old for it." Then, apparently feeling he might offend her, he added, "There's nothing wrong with surfing, of course. It's a great sport."

"I'd probably try it again if it fit my schedule better," Ellynne said. "I think it's hard because you have to surf at such odd hours."

"Yeah," Kip agreed, "a lot of guys spend a lot more time laying around on the beach talking about the big ones than actually getting up at five in the morning to catch them."

She thought of Kenny and his friends who seemed to talk about surfing a lot more than they actually did it. She had to admit that Kip was right.

"I just found other things. Anyway, school will start in three weeks and you'll be back to normal. Did you get all your reading done?"

"About half," Ellynne admitted. "But I'm determined to finish so I've started taking the books to the beach. I've also cut out television in the evening — no big loss."

"Any of the books good?"

"They all are," Ellynne answered. "Don't quote me, but I've really enjoyed every one of the books, especially the Henry James one. I know everyone complains about them but there's a reason why classics are classics."

They talked a few more minutes about school and then she said, "I have to go in now." Impulsively, she leaned over and planted a kiss on Kip's cheek.

Kip turned and tried to pull her closer so that he could really kiss her but she slipped quickly away and opened the car door. "See you soon," she said.

"Not till after Labor Day," Kip answered. "But you won't be able to get rid of me in September."

T welve

After their argument about the party, Kenny tried to be especially nice to Ellynne. He even offered to take her out to dinner one night, saying, "I found some money under my mattress. It was in an old sock that I think my father might have left behind."

"Use it to fix your car," Ellynne urged.

"It wasn't that much money," Kenny admitted. "Actually, some guy paid me twenty dollars for helping him move some furniture."

Ellynne sighed and said, "Kenny, when are you going to grow up?"

"We could go see the Muppets?" he was talking like his favorite three-year-old character now.

"Star Wars."

Kenny came to dinner at her house and they walked to the theater. It was a lot of fun, just being with him in the evening. As they walked along the street together, they held hands and he told her stories about his childhood escapades. Then he asked, "What about you? Didn't you ever get into any trouble? I'll bet you spent all the time running from little boys who chased you."

"I was kind of shy," Ellynne said.

"Sweet though," Kenny stopped and put his arm around her, kissing her on the street corner. She enjoyed the kiss partly because it seemed so special to actually be going somewhere with Kenny after dark. They stood quietly for a long time, looking at each other in the dim light of the street lamp. Kenny reached up and took her chin in his hand and said softly, "You mean a lot to me, Ellynne. More than you probably think."

She lifted her face to his for another kiss, allowing herself to sink into the soft, sweet feelings. "You mean a lot to me," she said as they pulled apart.

"I never really had a real girl before," Kenny said. His voice was soft and dreamy. "I guess I had lots of girls in a way, but none that I ever cared about. But you're different, Ellynne. You're a real person, and I can feel that you really love me. No one ever loved me before, I guess."

Ellynne was a little unnerved by what he said. Did she love him? She wasn't sure and anyway, she had a feeling he wasn't exactly thinking about romantic love. She decided to tease him by asking, "What about your mother? Your mother loves you, doesn't she?"

"Used to," Kenny said. "Used to think I was a great kid, but lately all I hear is complaints. By lately, I mean the last fifteen years or so." Then, as though he was sorry for saying so much, Kenny broke the mood. "We're late," he said and began to run. Ellynne ran after him and they laughed all the way to the theater. Kenny said, "Two senior citizens please."

The man at the box office didn't even smile as he stated the amount of the full-price tickets in an angry voice. When Kenny came back, holding the tickets in his hand, Ellynne said, "I wish you wouldn't do that."

"You're always after me to grow up."

They bought the biggest bucket of popcorn and sat near the front of the theater, reveling in the movie. When it was over Kenny said, "I forgot how much bigger things look on a movie screen."

"We can go see lots of others too," Ellynne said. She was quiet then, remembering that Kenny usually didn't have the money for movies. She didn't want to make him feel bad.

On the way home, they talked about the movie and then there were some long silences. He kissed her goodnight and she went inside the apartment alone. Once inside, she went to the kitchen and poured herself a glass of water. As she drank, she compared her movie date with Kenny to the one she'd had with Kip a few nights earlier. Funny how much she and Kip had found to talk about, but then she'd always been able to talk to Kip. Without accusing him, Ellynne began defending Kenny to herself in her own mind. *He's quite intelligent. It's just that his kind of intelligence doesn't make small talk.*

Satisfied that she'd explained things well enough to herself, she went to the bathroom to brush her teeth and get ready for bed. A few minutes later, the telephone rang and she picked it up, fully expecting it to be Kenny, who was probably home and calling to make some kind of joke.

It was Willie's voice who asked, "What would you give to be cheerleader?"

"What?" Not a very intelligent reply but all she could manage.

"Are you sitting down?"

Ellynne pulled a chair out from under the kitchen table and sat down. Her knees were weak just anticipating what Willie had to say. "Yes."

"I have some news," Willie said. "A woman came into the nursery today and ordered about two hundred dollars worth of plants. But she didn't want them delivered until September first, when she takes possession of her new house. So I'm filling out the order, not paying any particular attention until she gives me the address and it's Merri's house. Merri Merriweather is moving. Do you know what that means?"

"It means they'll have another tryout," Ellynne said. Her voice was shaking with excitement.

"It means we'll be on the team together after all."

"There will be other girls. I could lose again."

"You could win. You *will* win. Oh, Ellynne, I'm so excited I could cry. And guess what else?"

"What else?"

"Carl's coming home for two weeks. He decided to skip the last four weeks of summer school over there and just take a short tour. He's coming home to be with me."

"That's wonderful," Ellynne said.

"I get off work tomorrow at four," Willie said. "So I'll be at your house by four-thirty. We can practice till supper, O.K.?"

"Thanks Willie, but you'll be so tired," Ellynne said, "I've got the records, I can practice on my own."

"You need your old coach," Willie said. "Unless you'd rather not practice?"

"I have to practice," Ellynne said. "I'm really rusty."

"We sell some spray for that condition," Willie teased. "Want me to bring a bottle?"

"You really sure you'll have the energy?"

"If you can tear yourself from Mr. Wonderful, I've got the energy. Can you?"

"I want to be a cheerleader more than ever," Ellynne said. "I mean, I really *want* it."

"What about Mr. Wonderful?"

"He'll be happy for me if I make it."

"What about your mom? I'm pretty sure Judith still thinks being a cheerleader is silly."

Ellynne laughed and said, "Poor Mother. She's so worried about my dating Kenny that she'll probably be happy if I start spending my time practicing. When do you think they'll have the tryouts?"

"Probably as soon as Merri tells the school she's leaving."

"What if she doesn't?"

"What?'

"I mean what if they've just sold their house but they're moving down the block or something?"

"Nope. I asked the woman and she said Mr. Merriweather definitely had a big promotion and he was moving to Akron."

"Akron, Ohio," Ellynne said. "Poor Merri. I hope she doesn't have too hard a time in her new school."

"She'll get by."

"It's hard to start in your junior or senior year." Though she was sorry for Merri, she couldn't help being much more glad for herself. After all, Merri not only had never been her friend, but she had done everything she could to make Ellynne's start at Redondo High a difficult one.

Ellynne waited up for her mother to tell her the news.

Judith Aleese listened quietly and then

she said, "You didn't ask my permission and I guess I couldn't say no anyway, Ellynne, but the minute your school work drops, I'm warning you that you're coming off that team. Have you finished all the reading we agreed you'd do this summer?"

"I only have three more books."

"And three more weeks."

The three weeks went so fast that they seemed almost like a blur. Each day Ellynne rose early to do the housework, cook something for supper, and do some reading. About noon, she went to the beach to spend some time with Kenny and the group. By three-thirty, she had to leave if she was going to get her practicing time in so that she could get supper fixed and on the table, and Willie could get to bed early enough for her five o'clock alarm.

Kenny complained about how little he saw her, though she explained over and over how important the cheerleading competition was to her. He would listen, and when it was over he'd make some joke to indicate he understood but the next day, when she arrived a little late, or started to leave early, he'd complain again. After a week of that, she said, "You act like a kid, Kenny. Why can't you support me and my goals?"

"You're supposed to be my girl," he answered. "Why can't you hang around?"

Ellynne was furious as she accused, "You

don't want to understand what I'm saying because it isn't going your way. You're a spoiled brat."

"I love you, Ellynne. You're my girl and I want to spend time with you."

She stood stock still, staring at him. "Do you know what you just said? You said you loved me."

"I do," Kenny said. He was smiling at her, and she still wasn't sure whether he was teasing her. "I thought you knew that."

"No," she said slowly. "I thought you were just sort of fooling around. I didn't think you were serious about me."

"I'm serious," Kenny said. "And I'd like to be fooling around for real if you'd ever hold still."

This was the old Kenny, the joker that she was comfortable with. This was easier for her to deal with than the Kenny who declared his love. She laughed at him and stepped out of his reach.

But Kenny was in no mood to let himself be passed off as a joke today and he pulled her close, kissing her with more insistence than he'd ever shown before. He said, "I need you, Ellynne, and I want you beside me."

Ellynne sighed and shook her head. "If you really love me, you'll have to accept me the way I am. That means accepting the fact that there are some things I want in life."

"Me?" he was wearing one of his silly faces.

"Cheerleading. I want that so much. And good grades. And ... I don't know what else. Other things."

"There's more?" Kenny said, as though he found her very demanding. She wasn't sure whether he was kidding or not.

"I wish you could be more supportive," Ellynne said. "My mother says that the worst thing a woman can do is attach herself to a man who expects her to support his goals when he can't support hers."

"Do you support my goals?"

Ellynne groaned and wailed, "I would if I knew what they were! But I don't even know what you want in life."

"You."

She had an idea he wasn't entirely kidding. "It isn't enough," she said. "What about work?"

He jumped up, acted like he was having a fit and ran to the ocean, leaving her to stare at his retreating figure. She picked up her towel and book and started toward her bicycle. No matter how hard Kenny pushed her, she was going to practice her cheerleading and study her English. She was going to make sure her senior dreams came true.

*T*hirteen

They worked hardest on the jumps because Willie and Ellynne agreed that this was where she had lost out in the finals. Willie put it this way, "You've just got to think lightly. Like you're a bird and you can just leap. Ever watch ballet on TV?"

"Some."

"Ever see how those men leap up in the air? It's all positive thinking that lifts them. Close your eyes and think of flying."

"Like Tinkerbell," Ellynne laughed. "She said you had to believe in order to fly. But you know what? When I close my eyes I see a chubby little girl who's awful close to the ground."

"You are not chubby. You are just right."

"I've lost the pounds but not the mentality," Ellynne sighed. "Besides, it bothers me when I land. I keep wondering what Mrs. Bennet thinks."

"Who's Mrs. Bennet?"

"The lady who lives underneath us."

"We'll move to the beach."

"Oh no," Ellynne said.

"Sure," Willie said, "That's the perfect way to get you up in the air. You won't hurt yourself if you fall on the sand."

Against her better judgment, Ellynne allowed herself to be led to the beach below her house. Since it was so close to the pier, it was always crowded with tourists and there were usually a lot of little kids playing on the swing sets. Sure enough, by the time she'd done a few leaps, she had a large audience of two- to five-year-olds. "Pay no attention to them," Willie admonished, "you'll have to get used to crowds."

She jumped and jumped until she could jump no more. Then, wiping the sweat from her brow, she said, "I've had it for today. I'm not really in very good shape, I guess."

"You're in great shape," Willie assured her. "All that walking and running and bike riding has got your cardiovascular system up to perfection. And you're looking better on the jumps. Now let's try some handsprings and back bends."

"Oh no," Ellynne groaned but she did as she was told, paying careful attention to Willie's instruction.

Finally, Willie said, "My stomach is growling so it must be time to go. I'll see you to-morrow at four."

"You're a good teacher," Ellynne said. "Thanks."

Willie grinned and said, "I've got a lot at stake. With you on the team, it will be fun. Otherwise, it may be just a grind this year."

"What do you mean?" Ellynne wanted to be cheerleader so badly she couldn't imagine anyone finding it boring, especially the cheerful Willie who was never bored anyway.

Willie shrugged. "It's my second year and I don't have a boyfriend playing on the team or anything. I've never been that crazy about sports, and . . . it will just be a lot more fun for me if you're on the team, that's all."

"I'll do my best," Ellynne said.

"Best is always good enough," Willie answered, then she slapped her on the back and said, "Tomorrow we do Herkies."

"Ugh."

Judith was making the salad when Ellynne came into the apartment and Ellynne apologized. "It's all right," Judith said. " I don't care as much about the cooking as I do the schoolbooks. Did you get your reading done today?"

"Mostly." She had cut her study session short to get to the beach to see Kenny earlier because of the pressure he was putting on her, but she *had* studied when she got there.

"Good," Judith nodded and put the salad on the table. "Just as long as you can keep up your grade point average, I'll be delighted to see my girl in one of those silly little red skirts. You look great, by the way. I watched you out the window."

"Thanks." Ellynne didn't rise to her mother's caustic comments about the cheerleading uniforms. Judith had her opinions and she had her own. They agreed on a lot more matters than they clashed, so she knew she was lucky. Some girls in her class claimed they couldn't agree with their mothers about anything at all.

"I guess cheerleading keeps you in good shape. Wish I had time to exercise more." Judith sighed and continued, "In a way, I wish I'd waited till you went to college before I started law school. It seems like I'm so busy and we've grown so far apart. Maybe it would have been easier if I'd waited."

"No," Ellynne said. "It would have been worse."

"I suppose so," Judith sighed. "I suppose the worse thing I could have done is hang around and watch you all the time. The best role model I could be was to do something interesting on my own. Still, I hope we'll always be close. . . ." Judith took another helping of salad and waited for a response from Ellynne.

"We will be," Ellynne assured her mother. There were times when it seemed like their roles were reversed and she was older than her mother. Whenever that happened, it startled her. Now she looked at her mother and said, "You worry too much, you know."

"I suppose so. And I really am a workaholic," she continued. "But I'm trying, Ellynne, I'm really trying. Take this cheerleader obsession of yours. I've tried hard to understand that one but for the life of me, I can't see why a young woman in today's world would want. . . ."

Ellynne was almost laughing as her mother's apology slipped into another speech on the evils of cheerleading. It was interrupted by the telephone and Ellynne stood up quickly, hoping it was Kenny. She didn't recognize the voice on the other end who asked, "Ellynne? Ellynne Aleese?"

"Yes."

"This is Vicky Greenbaum. We met at the Wilsons'?"

"Yes." She remembered the woman now. She was the one who was so interested in the environment and she lived in San Diego.

"I'm coming up tomorrow for a few days. I'll be staying at the Wilsons', but I called you first because I know Willie is working this summer and you have more time. I hope you have *lots* of time because I want to get this whole thing started before school starts. That way, we can catch them while they are still enthusiastic about the beach. Nothing's as dead as a beach issue in December. You'd think it snowed in Southern California or something. Even adults aren't interested in the winter. Foolish of course, but that's the way volunteers are. Of course, you're an intelligent young woman who understands that the sea life exists in January as well as July. Aren't you?"

"Yes." Her mind was reeling from the speed with which Vicky talked.

"Good. Can you get me an executive board by six o'clock tomorrow evening? Your mother can serve as adult sponsor."

"An executive board for what?"

"S.T.B. That stands for Save The Beaches. I'm starting a statewide organization and the Redondo Beach chapter can be the first. I have the seed money and now I need the student power."

"What for?" Ellynne had the feeling she'd missed a vital part of the conversation.

"Why, we need the young people to save the beaches," Vicky said. "You were the one who gave me the idea, you know. At the party."

She racked her brain trying to think what she might have said at the party but she could think of nothing. "What did I say?" she asked finally.

"It wasn't what you said as much as your interested face," Vicky said. "And later Willie told me how you came here from the mid-west and loved the seacoast so much that you were spending your whole summer on the beach. I thought all the way home that night about how important it is to save the coastline for young people like you. So I started working on the project. Your mother had already said you and she would help and

I knew I could count on Willie. I've raised a little seed money and I have a couple of groups lined up in the San Diego area. I'll explain it all in detail tomorrow at the meeting. Seven o'clock at the Wilsons'?"

"What do you want me to do?"

"Invite your friends," Vicky said. "The group you spend your time at the beach with. And any other intelligent young people you can think of — high school and college students. Your mother too. See you tomorrow."

Vicky hung up so quickly that Ellynne suspected she might have been trying to avoid more questions or objections. Ellynne went back to the dinner table and said, "That was Vicky Greenbaum. She seems to think that you and I are going to spearhead a movement." She relayed the rest of the conversation to her mother and then asked, "What are we going to do?"

Judith looked at her daughter and asked, "That's sort of up to you, isn't it?"

"But what do you think?"

"I think it's a worthwhile cause. Not just saving the beaches, but the whole environment. Will your friends come to a meeting?"

"I'll ask," Ellynne said. "Kenny will probably do it if I insist. I'm not sure how many of the others."

It took the whole afternoon to persuade Kenny to go to the meeting with her. He kept saying, "I'm just not a political person," but eventually he agreed to pick her up at seven o'clock. As she had expected, the others just stared at her when she told them about the proposed meeting and suggested they might come. The only one who was even remotely interested in the project was Davy, who said he might come later if he finished his job on time. Davy was working as a dishwasher in a local restaurant and though his shift was over at seven, the other dishwasher was not always on time.

Since he had agreed to go to the meeting, Ellynne asked Kenny to join her and her mother for dinner that evening and he accepted the invitation. He rode his bicycle to her house at about four-thirty and watched her and Willie rehearse for the cheerleading tryouts for about an hour. When they were finished, the girls walked toward the boardwalk where Kenny sat on his bicycle seat.

"He is just about the most handsome man I've ever seen," Willie whispered as they came closer. "He is a real *doll*."

"He's really nice too," Ellynne said quickly. Why did she always feel she had to defend Kenny when someone commented on his looks? Why did she always feel that there was an edge of criticism in every compliment that Willie or her mother paid Kenny? Maybe it was because the only nice thing they ever said about him was the way he looked.

They were close enough to see Kenny's facial expression now and his blue eyes were filled with amusement as he asked, "How did you learn that thing? The one where you jump up and do the splits? I had no idea you were so talented."

"That's a Herkie," Ellynne said. "It's my secret talent, doing Herkies."

"I never even heard of Herkie," Kenny laughed. "Who is he?"

"How do you know it isn't a she?" Ellynne challenged. "I'm not sure what the name means, all I know is that's what you call it."

"Funny business," Kenny said. "I always thought all you had to do to be a cheerleader was to be a blonde beauty."

"Right now, our team is made up of two brown-skinned beauties," Willie said. "We're hoping Ellynne will supply the blonde balance."

"What else can you do?" Kenny asked Ellynne.

"Handsprings, jumps, cartwheels," Ellynne answered. "And I know all the cheers."

"Do one for me," Kenny said.

"No." Both girls were laughing.

"I won't go to your meeting unless you do a cheer."

Ellynne and Willie laughed and then Willie whispered to Ellynne who nodded. They stood on the beach and Willie counted, "One, two, three."

At three, they both jumped high into the air, clapped their hands and began jogging in place. As they jogged, they chanted, "K, E, N, N, Y." Then they repeated the chant but this time they did jumping jacks.

Then Willie marched alone while Ellynne did a series of cartwheels. At last, Ellynne and Willie shouted, "K, E, N, N, Y, he's our guy." They cheered and waved imaginary pompons and jumped in the air.

Kenny seemed both pleased and embarrassed by the cheer and he didn't tease them anymore about their skills. Instead, he shook his head and said, "I've got to get hold of a board for you. You've got the natural balance for surfing and I'm sure you can learn to be great at it."

"Next summer," Ellynne said. She felt as though, in some ways, this summer was over. There were only two more weeks until school started and she was so busy reading for school and practicing her cheers. Now if they got involved in this environment project, her time would really be taken up.

Kenny put his arm around her and hugged her close. "What's all this about next summer? We've got lots of time this year. Best beach weather of the year is September. You know it's the hottest month of all. Santa Ana winds too. That makes the ocean perfect for learning to surf."

"Santa Anas are when the winds come in off the desert instead of the ocean," Willie said. "It makes the coastline really hot, almost like the desert."

"Gets up to ninety degrees or above lots of times in September," Kenny assured her.

But Ellynne knew that no matter how hot the beach was, it wouldn't be the same for her after a day of school. She would be studying hard for grades, and if she was going to get that 4.0 average, she would especially need her weekends. She said to Kenny, "If I make cheerleader. . . ."

"You'll make it," Willie interrupted.

"If I make cheerleader," Ellynne repeated, "I'll be really busy at school. I won't have a lot of time for the beach."

"But there's after school, and weekends, and we can surf early in the mornings," Kenny protested. "I'll even get up at five to teach you."

Privately, Ellynne doubted that Kenny would do that, but she didn't argue. There was something a little sad about his eagerness. She put her hand on his arm and said, "You'll be in school and so will I. But we'll have time to see a lot of each other. Maybe in the evenings."

"You mean go on real dates?" Kenny asked.

His eyes were gleaming with mischief and Ellynne feared he was about to go into one of his silly acts. She laughed in advance and steered him toward the steps, saying, "We'd better go get the supper on the table or we won't get to the meeting on time." Turning to Willie, she asked, "Sure you won't stay?"

"Can't," Willie answered. "I have to help mom get ready for Vicky's meeting. And I'm waiting to hear from Carl."

"Is he here?" Ellynne asked.

"Girl, if he was here, would I be *here*?"

Willie asked. "I think he might call from New York today or tomorrow. At least I hope so."

As they climbed the stairs to the apartment, Kenny asked, "Carl's her boyfriend?"

"Yes," Ellynne answered. "He's a Stanford freshman — sophomore now. Name is Carl Robbins and he's very nice and very intelligent."

"You've met him, or is this just Willie's report?"

"I've met him twice. He *is* nice and he *is* intelligent. Quiet, though, and kind of shy. I get the impression he thinks he's really lucky to have found Willie because she can do his talking for him. Her mom and dad have an arrangement kind of like that."

"So Willie's boyfriend is just like her father. Freudian, no doubt. Am I anything like your father?"

Ellynne laughed loudly at the idea. She shook her head and asked, "Can you imagine my mother picking out someone like you?"

"Why not?" Kenny pretended to be insulted. "I'm a very intelligent youngster. Maybe I should ask your mother if she finds me attractive?"

"I wouldn't," Ellynne laughed, but then her mood changed and she said, "You know, I'm a lot like my mom in some ways."

"You don't find me attractive either?" Kenny raised his eyebrows in mock alarm and circled her with his arms. "But Matilda, I thought you were crazy about your Rudolph

. . . what has happened to us? Why are we drifting apart?"

"Be serious," Ellynne said and she pulled away from his grasp, but then she lifted her own arms and put them around his neck. "I just wanted to warn you that when school starts I turn into a different kind of person. I mean, I *am* ambitious and I *do* want to go to an Ivy League school. It's not just all my mom's idea."

"You're young," Kenny said. "You can change. You can kick this terrible work habit. You can learn to enjoy life. Put yourself in my hands and within a week I can turn you into a total winner. You can have it all, Ellynne, the sun, the moon, the stars."

"Sure Kenny, but I want more than that," Ellynne replied. She opened the door to the apartment, telling herself that she had tried to warn Kenny of what was coming. Even if he refused to listen to her, she had tried.

But once inside the apartment, Kenny drew her close to him and whispered in her ear, "Ellynne, I love you. I don't care if you are a straight A student and get to be President of the United States, I want to be your boyfriend. O.K.?"

"O.K." She smiled as he bent to kiss her, knowing that Kenny had heard her and understood. What was more, everything was going to work out just fine. She was going to be able to keep it all: her school grades, her cheerleading, and her wonderful boyfriend. Life was wonderful.

Fourteen

If Vicky Greenbaum was disappointed that there were only four people at the meeting, she gave no sign of it. She greeted Judith and Ellynne as though they were old friends and when Kenny was introduced she nodded her head and said, "Good. You look strong enough to be of some use to us."

Ellynne was pleased that Vicky seemed to be one woman who was more impressed by Kenny's potential strength than his good looks. She had the idea that Vicky put no thought to appearances at all, partly because Vicky was wearing an old pair of baggy pants and a sweat shirt. Across the front of the sweatshirt was the inscription, *Save The Whales*.

Vicky asked Willie to open the meeting and Willie did so with a straight face, but quickly introduced Vicky and turned it over to her. Vicky began by saying, "I want this organization to be run by young people, people like yourselves. I see it spanning the entire Pacific coastline within five years."

Vicky waited expectantly but no one said anything. So she continued, "These are the projects I had in mind, but there are many others. Think about what we could do with these." She took a list out of her sweatshirt pocket and said, "Dolphins in danger from tuna fishermen. Offshore oil drilling." Vicky continued to read from a long list. "So where shall we start?" she asked when she had finished.

"We need more people before we can do much of anything," Ellynne said. "I thought you had in mind something a lot simpler, like cleaning up the beaches."

"Good idea," Vicky said. "We'll begin there."

"But Vicky's right, the list of things to do is overwhelming," Judith said. "Maybe we should just get more people and have another planning session."

"If it is going to be an effective group, we'll have to *do* something," Ellynne began. "A lot of kids will understand picking up beer cans who won't understand legal issues."

They argued back and forth for a while and finally Willie said, "You two seem to think it's an either-or issue. Why can't we do both? We could organize a big cleanup day and pass out leaflets on issues at the same time."

"Then the kids who are cleaning up can

litter the beaches with the leaflets," Kenny interjected but no one laughed at his joke. Except for that, he was absolutely silent during the whole meeting.

They talked about a lot of things and finally agreed on a plan that started with putting up a booth in the local shopping mall and passing out leaflets. At that time they would try to collect the names of possible volunteers for a cleanup day.

Ellynne was impressed by the way Vicky went directly to the heart of an issue without any nonsense. Of course her mother had always been able to do that and so could Willie. Ellynne found she was really enthusiastic about working with such a group of forceful and intelligent people.

Vicky pointed to Ellynne and said, "You must be temporary chairperson because your mother and Willie are too busy." She didn't even seem aware that she had overlooked Kenny completely, but Ellynne was painfully aware of the fact that they had all been ignoring him for quite a while.

"If I'm chairperson, I'll begin by assigning you tasks. Willie, will you call everyone you can think of to see if they can help us *person* the booth?" Ellynne began. "Kenny, will you be in charge of building the booth?"

"How about a couple of wooden beer boxes and a surfboard for a table?"

"Will you?"

"Sure, Ellynne, it was just a joke."

They rode home in silence, each of them

lost in thoughts that apparently couldn't be shared. When they got to the apartment, Kenny said, "Got to be going. See you tomorrow."

"Thanks for coming," Ellynne said. "I appreciate it."

"Anything to please my girl," he answered and then he swung his leg over his bike and said, " 'Night, Judith."

" 'Night, Kenny. I'm glad you were there tonight."

Ellynne and her mother watched as Kenny pedaled away into the dark. Judith asked, "He's such a nice boy. Does he ever say anything serious?"

"Not often," Ellynne admitted.

"What's his home life like?"

"He lives with his mother. She's divorced. That's all I know."

Judith nodded her head and put her arm around Ellynne, saying, "I was proud of you tonight, but then I always am."

"It was fun working with you and Vicky. Willie too. But save your praise till we see how this whole thing comes out."

Ellynne ended up doing most of the work herself, just as she'd feared. Kenny insisted that a booth wasn't necessary and that they'd be better off with a simple card table. Since he was already angry because she spent so little time with him, she didn't push the issue, but simply said, "You may be right."

Willie's boyfriend Carl came to town the

next morning. Willie was much too distracted by the joy of seeing him to be any help at all. Actually, Ellynne volunteered to take over Willie's job and make some calls to other students herself. "I owe you one," she told Willie, "so run along and play with Carl."

She spent that evening on the phone, talking to people from school about the Save The Beaches project.

About nine-thirty she called Willie to tell her that she had a core group of ten who would be ready to go when school started. "I think that's enough, don't you?" Ellynne asked.

"I think we ought to get another ten from El Camino Junior College if we can," Willie said. "The high school kids will love that."

"Good idea."

"Can Kenny organize them?" Willie's voice was cautious.

"I'll check it out with him tomorrow."

"You might also check out whether he wants to doubt-date this weekend. Carl got tickets to a play in Los Angeles that his roommate's father wrote. We could have supper first. Fun?"

"Fun," Ellynne agreed. "I'll check with Kenny first thing tomorrow."

She almost had to chase Kenny down the beach to get him to answer her questions. Though she was annoyed, she tried to keep her voice light as she said, "Will you?"

"Will I what?"

"Will you organize the kids at El Camino? And will you go to the play with me?"

"No on both counts."

"Why not?"

"Why not what?"

She sighed and took his hand as they walked along the beach, "O.K. Let's take the play first. Why won't you go with me?"

"No bread."

"But Carl already has the tickets and I can pay for the dinner. I don't mind."

"I don't like closed-in spaces. Restaurants make me nervous."

"Well, why won't you organize the college? All you have to do is put an ad in the paper or something."

Kenny stood and faced her. His light blue eyes were clear and direct and his voice was steady as he said, "Ellynne, this is me, Kenny. Remember me? I'm not your ordinary high school sweetheart you can boss around. I'm me, and you may not like me the way I am, but I do. I don't want to change, Ellynne. I want to be exactly the way I was when you met me. Simple and sweet."

"I'm sorry." Then she shook her head and asked, "Why am I apologizing? What's wrong with wanting to go to a play? Or Save The Beaches? Why do I feel like there's something weird about my values when I'm around you?"

"Maybe because they're really not your values," Kenny said softly. "Maybe they're someone else's."

Fifteen

Carl invited Dr. and Mrs. Wilson to go to the play and Ellynne stayed home and watched television with Kenny. He seemed more comfortable spending time at the apartment now that he knew Judith better. Ellynne was glad about that because she had almost no time for the beach anymore.

Kenny grumbled a lot about missing her but he seemed to have decided that was the way things were going to be. She was careful to point out that acceptance went both ways and if he was going to be free to be himself, she would have to be also. Though she didn't insist, he said he was going to help during the Labor Day weekend even though he'd refused to try and organize a college group.

"Do what you really want," Ellynne urged. "I can live with it." He did show up at the shopping mall the first morning and met Carl, who was helping Willie pass out leaflets.

Kenny stayed almost three hours the first day but only about an hour the second. On the third day he just dropped by long enough to make a few jokes.

Willie and Carl held hands and seemed to be surrounded by a glorious pink cloud all the time they were together. Ellynne was happy for her friend. She thought being so far apart most of the time made their relationship more intense and exciting than it might have been if they'd been together all the time. On the night of the second day, she said something like this to her mother as they drove home from the mall. Judith had cheerfully volunteered her whole weekend to the S.T.B. Society.

"Maybe," Judith said, "but I think it puts a strain on things too. But they seem so happy with each other, I guess they'll manage no matter what."

"They're so different," Ellynne said, "but they don't ever fight."

"Being different doesn't necessarily mean fighting," Judith said.

"We fight because we're different."

"Or because we're the same," Judith teased. "Anyway, you don't fight with Kenny and he's certainly different from you."

She was surprised that her mother didn't know how often she and Kenny argued about things. Then she reminded herself that she was usually too busy defending him to her mother to talk about their arguments. "I fight more with Kenny than I did with Kip," she admitted.

"When's Kip coming home?" Judith asked.

"Today is his last day at Disneyland." She couldn't help but wonder if he would call her. Did she want to go out with Kip again? She felt like she wouldn't know until she heard his voice on the telephone. "He starts football practice tomorrow."

"School starts next week," her mother said. "Do you need new clothes?"

"I'll wait till it cools off," she said. Last year she'd learned that the first six weeks of school could be hotter than summer. Last year, she'd learned so much and this year she intended to benefit from that hard won education. She thought for a moment about the cheerleading competition. Would she win this time? Had she learned enough about it to get the position over the competition? She wasn't sure how many girls would try out but it was a good guess that Virginia Hanson would be there. She'd been a leading contender last year until she broke her ankle.

"You were so fussy about school clothes last year."

"I wasn't used to my new figure," Ellynne reminded her mother. "And I didn't have many leftovers." Besides, last year she had been hoping to find a boyfriend and this year the only men she was interested in would be in college, that is, if Kenny really enrolled. He swore to her that he was going, but she'd overheard him talking to Carl and he'd sounded a lot less definite.

"Maybe Kip will call tonight," Judith said. "I miss him."

"You said that."

"Well I do. Besides, I think Kip will probably organize S.T.B. at El Camino for us."

"Kip?" Ellynne was surprised at the thought. "He's always so busy with football and work."

"If you want something done, ask the busiest person you know." Judith added, "That's an old saying and it's pretty true."

"Maybe," Ellynne said doubtfully.

"Why don't you call him and ask him?" Judith suggested.

It finally dawned on her what her mother was up to. "Mother, I am not going to call Kip Russell the first night he's home. If he calls me later I'll tell him about S.T.B. and see if he's interested. But I'm not going to chase him just because you miss him."

"Just thought I'd try," Judith grinned and turned the car into their driveway. "It would be nice to see him though."

Kip didn't call that night or during the next week, but Ellynne wasn't disappointed. She was too busy sorting through the names and phone numbers they'd collected in the shopping mall, trying to organize a mailing list and make personal contact with people who had seemed really interested. Besides that, she was still reading for Senior English and practicing for her cheerleading contest one hour a day.

"I never see you," Kenny complained on Wednesday when she walked down to the Avenue C beach.

"You're seeing me now," Ellynne said. "And you could come by tonight."

"Party tonight."

"Oh, Kenny, I thought you were tired of those dumb parties."

"Want to come?" he asked.

"No."

Ellynne didn't bother to offer an explanation and Kenny didn't ask for one. Instead, he smiled and reached out to pull her close to him, saying, "You look pretty. I mean, you always look pretty but today you're beautiful. Like a girl who's in love. Are you in love, Ellynne?"

"I'm in love with a child," Ellynne said, "a nineteen-year-old who acts like he's about twelve." She was smiling as she kissed him but later, when they walked along the beach, she said seriously, "I worry about you, Kenny. Are you really going to enroll at El Camino?"

"Sure."

"And will you really go to classes?"

"Sure."

"I know you're a very intelligent person, Kenny, and I suppose in some ways you have the right idea about taking it easy in life. I mean, when I see the way some people run around in circles, then your way looks really sane. But Kenny, you don't want to end up a forty-five-year-old kid, do you?"

"Sure."

"What do you mean, sure? Have you been listening to me?"

"Sure."

They were silent after that, holding hands and walking along the beach together. Ellynne told herself to enjoy the day, as she had enjoyed her summer. But she could not escape the sense of closing that followed her as she walked along the water with Kenny and watched the infinite variety of dark lines that the water's edge made. *Summer's over,* she thought, and the idea almost made her want to cry.

"I was a really happy little kid," Kenny said suddenly. He laughed and said, "And that's what I'm going to be when I'm forty-five — a really happy kid."

"Everyone has to grow up, Kenny."

"That's what you think," he said. Then he shouted, "Last one in's an outlander. Let's swim."

"I have to go back now. Willie's coming to help me with my cheerleader practice."

"Skip it today."

"I can't. She's giving up time with Carl to help me and I'd feel terrible if I stood her up."

"Then kiss me good-bye," Kenny demanded, pursing his lips and acting like a three-year-old who was saying goodbye to his grandmother. "Come on, Ellie, give us a kiss."

Laughing, she kissed Kenny good-bye and started home. Turning once, she saw his bronze body diving into the water. As always, she felt good just looking at him. *I guess I really do love him,* she thought, but behind that feeling of love there was a soft ring of sadness.

Kip called her that evening and she invited him over, telling herself that he was an old friend whom she hadn't seen all summer. He brought his new John Lee Hooker record and they listened to that and talked about their summers. She told him all about her cheerleading practice and the S.T.B. Society.

"I want you to meet Kenny," she said. "I mean, you'll both be going to the same school and you might be friends. He's really a nice guy."

"I'm sure he is."

Kip's voice carried conviction and Ellynne was surprised. She said, "Really?"

"Of course he's nice, Ellynne. I don't think you would have fallen for some guy who wasn't very special. I mean, you fell for me didn't you? And I'm special."

"Yes you are, but I'm not sure I can give give you what you want," Ellynne said.

"Let me decide that," Kip said.

Sixteen

The first week of school was the fastest week of Ellynne's life. After school on Friday, she attended a meeting for girls who had hopes of becoming cheerleaders; she learned the tryouts would be the following Tuesday.

"Didn't give you much time, did they?" Judith asked when she and Ellynne were having Saturday morning breakfast.

"It's because our first football game is Friday afternoon," Ellynne said. "They want the whole thing settled fast."

"You should have a big advantage," Judith predicted. "You and Willie have certainly practiced hard enough."

"Virginia Hanson's been practicing, too," Ellynne said. "I heard today that Merri spent a lot of time coaching her before she left town. Merri probably hated the thought of me taking her place."

"I'm more worried about your grades than

anything," Judith said and Ellynne wondered if her mother thought that was news.

"I think I aced the test in English," Ellynne assured her mother. "I was the only one who'd really read the assignment. The teacher's very demanding. He gave us fifty pages to read in one night. And I guess that's going to be typical."

"That's two hours a night. You'll have to put a lot of hours in on weekends if you're going to keep up. Looks like I won't be the only workaholic around here this year."

"I'm going to the beach today."

Ellynne was prepared for a fight but her mother only said, "Have fun. I'm going to study."

"Then this evening Kenny and I are going out."

Judith raised an eyebrow and said, "That's nice."

"And tomorrow afternoon I'm going to Los Angeles with Kip," Ellynne said. "We're going to hear a blues concert at the museum."

"That's nice." There was a lot more enthusiasm in her tone of voice this time but she asked, "And when will you study?"

"Right now," Ellynne said, and rose from the breakfast table and went right to her room to crack open the books. If she was going to balance her life and have everything she wanted, she would have to learn to use every minute to its fullest advantage. She would have to schedule her activities.

* * *

Tuesday afternoon came quickly and El-lynne barely had time to worry about the outcome of the tryouts until she went into the gym itself. Once inside, she felt the same nervousness and need that she'd been full of last year. *I really want this,* she realized as she stood on the sidelines and watched the other girls try out.

She was one of the last ones called and by the time her turn came, she felt like she'd forgotten everything she thought she'd learned. But then the music began and she saw Willie standing across the room, raising her arms in a victory signal. She knew that Ellynne had worked hard for this second chance. Ellynne took a deep breath and bounced out on the floor.

She went through her whole routine, start-ing with the jumps, doing her cartwheels and ending with the Herkies. As far as she could tell, she didn't miss a beat and she kicked as high as she'd ever been able to be-fore. By the time she was finished she wasn't sure she'd won but she was *sure* she'd done a good job. The whole thing took only a few minutes but when it was over, she was pant-ing and wiping sweat off her brow.

Willie was grinning broadly, so Ellynne guessed that she must have been very good — at least she hoped so. She knew that Vir-ginia and possibly one of the other girls had as much natural talent as she did, so it was partly a matter of showing off to her best advantage.

168

There were only ten girls who tried out and it took less than an hour. The coach said if they wanted to, they could wait for the decision. Then the coach and her two helpers conferred for a few minutes in the gym office. As they waited, Willie said to Ellynne, "I never saw you look better."

"Virginia looked good too."

"Virginia's good, but you're better. Last year I wasn't so sure about that but this year I think you could have beaten Merri — you were that good."

The coach came out just then and said, "It's Ellynne Aleese."

Willie and Ellynne jumped up and down and hugged each other in glee. Then the other girls managed to crowd around and congratulate her. Ellynne felt as though she was floating when she and Willie walked out of the gym and down the street.

Ellynne was nervous as she prepared to perform for the first football game on the next Friday night. As they were getting off the bus, she said, "I hope I don't get sick or fall down or anything."

"You won't," Marsha assured her.

"You may," Willie said with a teasing voice, "but remember that you just have to get up and get going again. The show must go on. The whole team is depending on you."

"Do you really believe that?"

"Yes I do," Willie answered. "At least, I think it helps them a lot when we whip the audience into a frenzy. All those cheers work like extra adrenaline for the players. There've been studies on it."

"You're making me more nervous," Ellynne complained. "Now if we lose I'll feel it was my fault."

"Maybe it will be," Willie said.

"Willie, don't be so mean," Marsha said. Then she added to Ellynne, "Just do your best and don't worry too much. They won't even know if you make a mistake."

"Unless I slip and fall," Ellynne said, but just saying her fears out loud had helped her a lot. She checked her appearance in the mirror of the locker room and had to admit that she looked pretty good. Her cheeks were rosy red and her eyes were shining with excitement as she looked back at herself. She said aloud to her reflection, "Congratulations kid, you finally made the grade."

Then she turned and followed Marsha and Willie out to the football field bleachers where they would wait for the crowd to finish filing into the stadium. Once she was seated and waiting, Ellynne was really more excited than nervous. Her excitement kept her from worrying too much about making a mistake — she just kept going over the various moves in her mind. Then the players ran out onto the field and it was time for them to begin. She took her place between Willie and Marsha and looked up at the crowd.

The faces of the crowd looked like a lot of

round, shiny circles staring down at her and she was reminded more of light bulbs than of people as she looked back at them. She couldn't make out anyone she knew and that made her feel more and less comfortable at the same time. It was good she couldn't see her mother, who she knew was sitting somewhere on the bleachers with Dr. and Mrs. Wilson and Carl. Yet she wished she could see well enough to know whether Kenny had come to the game as he'd promised.

They kept the cheers simple until half-time and then they moved into the more complicated routines. By the time they were in the third quarter, Ellynne was relaxed enough so that she was ready for anything. When Willie asked, "How about some cartwheels?" she nodded her head yes. So Marsha and Willie chanted and jumped as they waved their pompons, and Ellynne did a series of cartwheels that lasted at least two minutes. When she finished, she bowed to the applause.

It started to rain the last few minutes of the fourth quarter and Redondo High lost the game, so the evening was not exactly a total success. Even so, Ellynne left the football field feeling very proud of herself. She'd discovered that she loved performing and that she wasn't at all shy anymore, at least not while she was wearing that short red skirt and surrounded by her friends.

As they were dressing in their regular clothes, Marsha said, "What did I tell you? Piece of cake?"

"Piece of cake," Ellynne agreed. "I loved it."

She told her mother the same thing later that evening. "I'm glad you got it," her mother said. "You look absolutely glowing with happiness. I'm so happy for you."

"I think I'm a ham," Ellynne said. "I loved the applause when I did the cartwheels."

"Everyone likes to be appreciated," Judith said. "There's nothing wrong with accepting well-deserved applause. Besides, those cartwheels were really spectacular. Kip thought so too."

"Was Kip there?"

"Didn't you see him?"

"I couldn't see anyone," Ellynne admitted.

"He sat beside me the whole time," Judith said.

"Why didn't he stick around and say hello?"

"I think that might have been my fault," Judith said. "I thought you said that Kenny would be there and I told Kip so he wouldn't be uncomfortable. But then Kenny didn't show up and you missed out on Kip's company. I'm sorry."

"It's all right," Ellynne said. "It's not your fault." She was surprised at how disappointed she was though. It would have been nice to hear Kip's congratulations.

She found herself washed back in time to last year, when she'd lost the cheerleader tryouts. As she thought about how supportive Kip had been and how crazy she'd been about him, she wondered how she had lost that wonderful feeling. Sadness almost spoiled her mood as she grieved for her lost love. And Kenny, the man she now loved, hadn't even bothered to come to the game!

But it was Kip, not Kenny that she missed seeing. After all, he had suffered with her when she didn't make the squad last year. She and Kip went back a long way together and it would have been nice to share her triumph with him.

Seventeen

Ellynne felt as though she were stretched very thin by her activities during the next few weeks. Despite her confidence in her schoolwork and the fact that she was ahead of the others in English, she found she had to study hard to keep getting those A's she was aiming for. Her cheerleading took up a lot of time after school and her late Friday nights made her very tired on Saturday mornings. On top of that, she was still working hard on the S.T.B. Society.

Vicky came to town early in October to help them plan for their next activity — the El Camino Homecoming weekend. The girls explained to her that they were having trouble finding volunteers to help them.

"Kip, that's a friend of mine, said he'd help as much as he can but he works almost full time and really isn't on campus much. Besides, he's playing football during that weekend. He has to practice and work so he's not really going to be around," Ellynne explained.

"We've asked a lot of other people but excuses are easy to find, I guess," Willie added.

Vicky let them complain a little while longer and then she yawned to indicate she was bored. "It's the same the world over," Vicky said. "A few people do all the work."

"There are kids at the high school who'll help," Ellynne said, "but we really need college people to be in the booth that weekend. They aren't going to listen to high school kids. Besides, the booths are only supposed to be for college organizations."

"What about that boy who came to the first meeting?" Vicky asked. "Such a nice young man."

"He hasn't been a lot of help," Ellynne admitted. "He's not a very political person."

"But he'll probably help you if you ask him," Willie said. "Ask him to make it a personal favor."

"That's the way," Vicky said. "For a pretty girl like you, he'll do it. Tell him you really need him. No man can resist being needed."

"Kenny can," Ellynne said. Then she added, "I'll try."

She was having trouble finding time to spend with Kenny these days and their relationship was more strained than she wanted to admit, even to herself. But fitting

Kenny into her busy schedule was sometimes impossible, especially since he never really wanted to do anything but go to the beach and watch television.

The funny part was that she'd been seeing almost as much of Kip as she was of Kenny. True to his word, Kip had been around quite a bit, either dropping by for a cup of coffee on his way to work at the supermarket or stopping into school to say hello. Kip had even come to a couple of other football games and taken her out for a Coke later.

These days she couldn't help but find a whole lot more things to talk to Kip about than she could Kenny. She still loved Kenny, of course, but Kip and she did have a lot in common. . . .

"So what do you think?" Vicky asked and Ellynne realized she'd allowed her mind to drift completely away from the subject. Blushing because she'd been busy dreaming about boys instead of sticking with the business at hand, she said, "I guess I wasn't listening."

"Kenny will build the booth on Friday morning. We'll get there after school and start passing out leaflets to kids who are building other booths. Maybe we can pick up some volunteers."

"Good idea."

They adjourned the meeting and Ellynne went directly to the beach. She found Kenny lying in the warm sunshine, staring up at the blue sky. He didn't hear her come up behind him and when she said his name softly, he sat up quickly, as though he was startled. "Hi, Ellynne. You look funny with all those clothes on. Like an outlander."

"I didn't have time to change and I have to get home. I came by to ask a favor."

"Ask away."

"Will you build a booth for us at El Camino next weekend? For the homecoming thing. They're letting all the campus organizations hand out publicity. Right by the hot dog stands. Can you do it? Maybe get Davy to help you?"

"I guess so."

"Here's a fifty dollar check made out to the Lumberyard. We've spent nearly all the money Vicky gave us to start with but we can afford to buy the lumber for the booth. Do you think you can borrow tools? Will that be enough money? It just needs to be a simple booth — nothing fancy."

"A surfboard and a couple of boxes?"

"No, a small cage to keep you in. And I need you to be there Friday night and all day Saturday. We desperately need an El Camino student to be legal. Besides, you know how people are. College kids won't want to talk to high school kids." The words tumbled out of her mouth.

"O.K." Kenny reached up and took her hand, pulling her down on the sand beside him. "And for all that I get a kiss?" He bent her over slightly and she found she was leaning back into his arms. His lips closed softly over hers and she sank into the sweet softness of his embrace.

"You're my girl," Kenny said and he kept his arms closed around her.

She sat quietly for a while, enjoying being close to Kenny, enjoying the peaceful quality of the beach on a day when there were so few people around. It gave the beach and the ocean an even more beautiful quality to be there with just the natural world. "I'm glad we cleaned things up. Looks a lot better, doesn't it?"

"Always looked fine to me."

Ellynne sat still and said no more until the sun began to get redder and she realized it was getting later. Then she jumped up and said, "I'm late. I've got to go. See you tonight?"

"Don't know," Kenny said. "There's this guy that Sailor knows who might help me fix my car."

Ellynne tried to keep the impatience out of her voice as she said, "Well if I don't see you before then, see you Friday. Don't let me down, Kenny."

"You can count on me."

Kenny didn't come over that night but Kip did; he stopped by with a new blues record under his arm and suggested she might like to listen to it. "Come on in," Ellynne said, "but I'll warn you that I'm in a kind of crazy mood."

They listened to the record and talked and Kip asked, "So why crazy?"

"I've got too much to do," Ellynne said. "And the sickening part of it is that I want to do it all. I mean, I really want to make straight A's and I really want to be a cheerleader and I really want to be president of S.T.B., at least until it gets a good start."

They talked more about the group and Kip's new school until Judith came home.

Kip stood up, saying, "I'd better go. I have to be at the supermarket at eight in the morning. 'Night, all."

"I'll walk out with you," Ellynne said. She followed him to the door and once outside, Kip kissed her on the cheek and said, "I'm not having nearly as much fun as I would be if we were still together."

Ellynne laughed and stepped back, "We see a lot of each other."

"But your heart belongs to someone else," Kip reminded her. "Or does it?"

"Yes it does," Ellynne said in a voice that was much firmer than she really felt.

"One of these days you'll change your mind," Kip said.

". . . And you'll be gone," Ellynne finished his sentence for him.

Kip shook his head and said, "I was going to say, and we'll live happily ever after." He bent down and kissed her lips, swiftly, lightly, as though he was afraid to frighten her away. "I'll be there," he whispered, "you can count on me."

Eighteen

Friday morning brought Santa Ana wind conditions and Ellynne dressed in her lightest cotton blouse and skirt. Even so, she was sweating by the time she'd walked to school. Later in the day, as the temperature rose to 97 degrees, Ellynne's nervousness increased.

At lunch, Willie asked, "Weather got you down?"

"Something like that." She didn't even want Willie to know what she was worrying about. It would be time enough to find out if her suspicions were accurate when they left there that afternoon. But even as she ate her tuna salad sandwich and drank her lemonade she was making emergency plans.

Willie had her mother's car that day so they could drive directly over to El Camino after school. As they got in the car, Willie said, "If by any chance Kenny hasn't built the booth. . . ."

Ellynne realized that Willie had the same fear she did — that the hot weather had been too tempting and Kenny had skipped off to the beach. "If he hasn't built the booth, we can use two card tables and Judith will fill in for him," Ellynne said.

Willie looked at her expectantly.

"And I'm going to break off with him," she added in a quiet but determined voice.

"You wouldn't."

"I would."

The silence in the car was heavy after that and Ellynne was grateful that Willie didn't probe her feelings more closely. It was good to have a friend who didn't need to have explanations in order to understand you.

When they got to the football stadium they could hear the sound of hammers and saws as soon as they got out of the car. Ellynne was holding her breath as she rounded the corner and looked down the long row of booths that were being built. She didn't see any bronzed bodies and knew immediately that Kenny was not there.

"Maybe he came early and he's finished," Willie said.

Ellynne allowed herself to be led down the long row to the end but there was no sign of Kenny. There was one booth that was almost finished though, and there were no people around it. "Maybe this is our booth," Willie said. "Maybe he's just gone for a Coke or something."

"That's a woman's briefcase there." Ellynne pointed to a soft gray briefcase exactly like the one her mother carried. Then beside it she saw a tee-shirt that had a picture of Mickey Mouse on it. "It's our booth though," Ellynne said, with tears of gratitude coming to her eyes.

Behind them, Judith Aleese's voice said, "Hi. We just stopped for a ten minute break and you caught us loafing."

"Want a Coke?" Kip asked, as he offered his, "I'll go get two more."

"No thanks," Willie said. "We've only got a couple of hours before our game so we'd better get to work. How come you two are here?"

"It was so hot in Los Angeles that I couldn't stand it anymore," Judith said. "Besides, I had an idea that you might be in a jam. But when I got here, Kip already had half the booth built."

"I thought you had to work every day this week?" Ellynne asked Kip.

"I switched schedules," Kip said. "Figured you might need me, and I wanted you to know I meant it when I said you could count on me."

"I already knew that," Ellynne said. "But you certainly saved the day for S.T.B. Mom, can I use your car?"

"Sure. Where are you going?"

"To the beach," Ellynne said. "I'll get back as soon as I can but I have something I have to do."

"To the beach? You don't mean you're

going to leave us . . . ?" Judith's objections
were stopped when both Kip and Willie shook
their heads in warning. She handed Ellynne
the keys without another word.

Ellynne drove swiftly, keeping her mind
as clear and uncluttered as she could; she
wanted to do this as quickly and cleanly as
she could and she wasn't going to let herself
get worried by second thoughts. But when
she parked the car and walked down the steps
to the Avenue C beach, her heart caught with
a sadness. She realized that even if Kenny
and she never saw each other again he would
always occupy a special place in her heart.

She could see him from this distance,
standing up on his surfboard and riding in
on the crest of a wave. She stood on the sand
and waved to him, motioning for him to come
all the way in. He caught sight of her and
tumbled off the board into the water, and
then he was wading into shore, grinning as
he greeted her. "Did you ever see such off-
shores? Santa Ana does it every time. Offshore waves all day long and perfect surfing
weather. No school — so we had the beach
to ourselves."

"You've been here all day?"

"Sure. Since five this morning. First thing,
when I heard the weather forecast, I knew
it was my day. My perfect day. And it has
been. Go home and get your suit. I'll give you
a surfing lesson."

"I've got a game tonight and there's the
booth at the El Camino homecoming week-

end," Ellynne kept her voice steady as she explained.

"Oh, yeah, I forgot. Sorry about that. But I wouldn't have missed this for anything. Perfect waves."

"I figured."

"Come on, Ellynne, don't be mad."

"I'm not mad," Ellynne said. "That's the funny thing about it. I'm really not mad. And in a way, I think I'll always love you. You were good for me and I had a great time this summer. I wouldn't have missed *that* for the world. But summer's over and I'm not going to see you anymore."

"I said I was sorry. What more do you want?"

"I want to break up with you, Kenny." Ellynne's voice was quiet and she hoped he wouldn't notice that she was on the verge of tears. She knew that she was doing the right thing and she didn't want Kenny to try to talk her out of it. She held her chin up high and forced herself to look him in the eyes. She was shocked by the expression on his face. Kenny looked angry and even a little frightened, but he said, "Don't be such a baby. Just because I didn't make your silly little booth you're going to take your toys and go home." He was talking in his three-year-old character's voice again, but this time, his voice was dripping with sarcasm.

"It's not just because of today, Kenny," Ellynne said. "We were never right for each other. It was fun while it lasted but I guess I've just outgrown you."

"You haven't outgrown anything," Kenny said, practically shouting. "You're just stupid. And don't tell *me* about fun. You don't know anything about fun."

"Yes, I do, Kenny, and I'm not stupid," Ellynne answered. "I'm a balanced person. Something you'll never understand."

"I know this wasn't your idea," Kenny said, after a moment. "Your mother never liked me."

"Judith liked you," Ellynne said. "And I'm making my own decisions. Good-bye."

Kenny stood there with his surfboard under his arm. The sun was shining on the little beads of salty water that glistened on his shoulders and face and he looked like he was encrusted with small jewels. He shrugged and said, "See you around, Ellynne. Maybe next summer."

"No." Ellynne said. "I said I've outgrown you, and I meant it." She turned and walked off the beach without looking back.

By the time she got back to El Camino the booth was in place and Judith said, "We can all go get a hamburger before we go our separate ways. I guess Kenny won't be working the booth tonight?"

"No," Ellynne said. Then she laughed and said, "Last time I saw him he looked like a Greek god risen from the sea. Covered with jewels." She realized the others didn't know what she was talking about and she said, "I mean there were little salt water drops all over him and the sun was shining on them so they looked like jewels — pearls or something." It was hopeless, she decided. None of them would ever understand what Kenny had meant to her. In some ways, she didn't understand it herself. "Let's eat," she said.

She rode to the restaurant with Kip; Willie and Judith both took their own cars so it would be easy to separate after supper. Judith would be at the booth that evening and Kip would work till midnight at the supermarket. Willie and she would be leading cheers, helping the Redondo High football team fight for their first victory.

As they drove together, Kip asked, "What happened at the beach?"

"I broke up with him."

"For good?"

"Yes."

"Does that mean anything for us?"

"I hope so, Kip. But, I don't know. We could try."

"I'd like that. But if you dump me again, Ellynne, that's it. It hurt too much."

"I understand and I'm sorry, Kip," Ellynne said gently. "It's hard to explain what happened, but this summer was important to me in a lot of ways." She thought of Kenny as she'd last seen him; he really was handsome and a lot of fun. Ellynne wondered if she would miss him. Yes, probably some, she decided, but not that much.

They pulled into the parking lot and Kip turned off the ignition as he turned to face her. He said, "You don't have to explain, Ellynne. I don't need explanations. All I need to know is that you're with me again."

"I'm with you," Ellynne said and put her arms around Kip's neck, drawing him closer to her. She lifted her face for a kiss and he pressed his lips closer to hers, at the same time he drew her into his embrace.

The old magic was back, Ellynne realized. She felt as if she had been under a spell and had suddenly been released, awakened after a long dream. She sighed and stirred in his arms, saying, "I think it was really you I loved all along. I was just bewitched for a little while."

"That's what I think too," Willie's voice said from outside the car.

Ellynne and Kip pulled apart, laughing at having been caught by Willie and Judith. Ellynne was trying to find something to say when Judith said with mock severity, "Stop that silliness and come on in. We've got a million things to do tonight."

"Maybe so," Ellynne answered, "but then again, maybe we just did the most important one."

She turned to Kip who smiled and said, "We've got plenty of time." Then he kissed her again.

Ellynne sighed with happiness. Her senior year was turning out to be a dream come true.

WILDFIRE®

Move from one breathtaking romance to another with the Premier Teen Romance line!

NEW WILDFIRES! $2.25 each

- [ ] QI33096-9 **CHRISTY'S LOVE** Maud Johnson
- [ ] QI32536-1 **KISS AND TELL** Helen Cavanagh
- [ ] QI32846-8 **NICE GIRLS DON'T** Caroline B. Cooney
- [ ] QI33490-5 **PHONE CALLS** Ann Reit

BEST-SELLING WILDFIRES! $1.95 each

- [ ] QI32540-X **BROKEN DREAMS** Susan Mendonca
- [ ] QI32371-7 **CALL ME** Jane Claypool Miner
- [ ] QI32359-8 **CLASS RING** Josephine Wunsch
- [ ] QI31252-9 **GOOD-BYE, PRETTY ONE** Lucille S. Warner
- [ ] QI32558-2 **HOLLY IN LOVE** Caroline B. Cooney
- [ ] QI32003-2 **JUNIOR PROM** Patricia Aks
- [ ] QI32431-4 **LOVE GAMES** Deborah Aydt
- [ ] QI32535-3 **ON YOUR TOES** Terry Morris
- [ ] QI32002-5 **SECRET LOVE** Barbara Steiner
- [ ] QI32538-8 **SPRING LOVE** Jennifer Sarasin
